**"We have to get out of here,"
Pastor Dev said seriously.
"Lydia, are you with me?"**

He said it right up close to her, his eyes a clear, beautiful blue as he looked at her. Only she couldn't make out what was going on in his mind. "I'm with you," she whispered, thinking she'd follow him to the ends of the earth if he asked. "But I sure would like to know why we're getting out of here. We should call the police. We should—"

"No police," he said firmly. "I'll explain everything later," he added, his voice softer, his fingers brushing through her bangs.

Suddenly she realized that despite the danger—despite the confusion—this was the very thing she'd dreamed of: his running his fingers through her hair.

LENORA WORTH

grew up in a small Georgia town and decided in the fourth grade that she wanted to be a writer. But first she married her high school sweetheart, then moved to Atlanta, Georgia. Taking care of their baby daughter at home while her husband worked at night, Lenora discovered the world of romance novels and knew that's what she wanted to write. And so she began.

A few years later, the family settled in Shreveport, Louisiana, where Lenora continued to write while working as a marketing assistant. After the birth of her second child, a boy, she decided to pursue her dream full-time. In 1993, Lenora's hard work and determination finally paid off with that first sale. "I never gave up, and I believe my faith in God helped get me through the rough times when I doubted myself," Lenora says. "Each time I start a new book, I say a prayer, asking God to give me the strength and direction to put the words to paper. That's why I'm so thrilled to be a part of Steeple Hill's Love Inspired line, where I can combine my faith in God with my love of romance. It's the best combination."

SECRET
AGENT
MINISTER

Lenora Worth

Steeple
Hill®

Published by Steeple Hill Books™

STEEPLE HILL BOOKS

Steeple
Hill®

ISBN-13: 978-0-373-44258-4
ISBN-10: 0-373-44258-0

SECRET AGENT MINISTER

Copyright © 2007 by Lenora H. Nazworth

This edition published by arrangement with Steeple Hill Books.

® and TM are trademarks of Steeple Hill Books, used under license.
Trademarks indicated with ® are registered in the United States Patent
and Trademark Office, the Canadian Trade Marks Office and in other
countries.

www.SteepleHill.com

Printed in U.S.A.

Do they not go astray who devise evil? But mercy
and truth belong to those who devise good.
—*Proverbs* 14:22

To Merline Lovelace and the participants
of her workshop Four Steps to Perfect Plots
at the 2006 Written In The Stars NOLA STARS
(North Louisiana Storytellers and Authors)
conference. Thanks to all of you for
giving me this story idea!

And special thanks and acknowledgment to
paratroop and skydiving instructor Jim Bates at
aero.com for his help on how to "let go of a plane."
Any mistakes were my own!

ONE

Someone was going to have to explain about the dead body in the bathtub. *Really*. That thought kept running through Lydia Cantrell's head as she looked from the grotesque body of a wide-eyed dead man wearing a bloody suit to the shock-filled stare of the surprised and *very alive* man standing in front of her.

Then her practical mind went into overdrive. She would probably have to explain how she'd wound up in Pastor Dev's hotel room late at night, only to find him wearing a bright red action figure T-shirt and old, faded jeans, while staring at the body in the tub, his expression filled with shock and something else Lydia couldn't quite figure out, something that looked like anger and resolve. Since she'd never seen Pastor Dev angry, she couldn't grasp what was happening or the strange look she saw in his deep blue eyes.

And she certainly couldn't grasp his attire. Lydia rarely saw Pastor Devon Malone dressed in anything other than a nice suit and interesting tie, so she was a bit taken aback, seeing him in jeans and a T-shirt and realizing that the man was built like a regular weight lifter and football jock all rolled into one mighty good-looking package. That, and the body in the tub, really set Lydia into a tizzy.

But she *had* come here for a reason. A very legitimate reason. They were supposed to go over Pastor Dev's notes for his speech the next day. They were attending a statewide religious conference in Atlanta, Georgia. That's why Lydia was in his hotel room tonight—to help him go over his notes and make sure his speech was tip-top.

Pastor Dev was funny that way. He was thorough and very detail-oriented. He liked to do things the right way. Some implied he was a perfectionist, but Lydia called that just plain hardworking and dedicated. That's why the man was such a good minister. His speech, entitled "Pastoral—Finding Inner Peace in a Troubled World" would, of course, be excellent. Everything about Pastor Dev was excellent, in Lydia's mind, at least. Which was why she refused to believe there was a dead man in the room, or that Pastor Dev had anything whatsoever to do with it.

Closing her eyes to the image of the dead man, Lydia thought about how people would react to a young, impressionable girl of twenty-five visiting a single man's hotel room late at night, but she kept telling herself this was all beyond reproach—if you didn't count murder, of course. This was Pastor Dev after all. Even the church matrons who'd ridden the bus up to Atlanta with them had given this meeting their blessings. Because they knew Lydia and the pastor had work to do—God's work. And because Pastor Dev was always a perfect gentleman. Everyone knew that.

And there had been a chaperone present—Pastor Dev's roommate. Except his roommate and mentor, Pastor Charles Pierson from Savannah, was in no shape to chaperone, since he was the dead man in the bathtub.

Lydia thought about all the people who had put their trust in Pastor Dev and her. This certainly wouldn't sit well with the church members back home in Dixon, Georgia. It was where Pastor Dev preached and Lydia worked as his secretary ever since she'd come back with a business degree from the University of Georgia.

And she'd worked hard to get the job at the First Church of Dixon, because she had decided instead of building a career in some big company with stock options and a great 401K plan, she wanted to work for Pastor Dev. She'd fallen in love with him one Christmas during her senior year at UGA, when she'd met him at her parents' annual Christmas Eve open house. He was the new preacher, single and just a few years older than Lydia. And he was so good and sweet and kind, she knew immediately that he was the man she wanted to spend the rest of her life with.

Only, he still didn't know that. Because, though Lydia made goo-goo eyes at him all the time and twirled her long, dark blond hair each time he came to stand by her desk back in the church office, he'd never once noticed a thing about her or her feelings. He was always too preoccupied with taking care of church members—he was so very dedicated that way.

Lydia felt safe with Pastor Dev. He was such a mild-mannered, quiet man, and she just knew she was perfectly safe with him even now, with that horrible body staring up at them.

But she had to admit things looked mighty suspicious with Pastor Dev standing there all shocked and surprised and looking from the body back to her with a kind of dread.

Finally, Lydia managed to speak. "I know you didn't kill that man, Pastor Dev. Please tell me you didn't kill your roommate?"

"Of course I didn't do this, Lydia," he replied, a soft plea in his words. Then he just stared at the body, that strange look on his face.

While she waited for an explanation, Lydia reminded herself that Pastor Dev was so quiet and focused, so kind and polite, so good and solid, that he could never lift a hand in brutality or violence toward another human being. The man was a walking example of what being a true Christian was all about. Period. End of discussion.

So, Lydia asked another question. "If you didn't kill your friend, then who did?"

Devon Malone heard the doubt in Lydia's appeal. And because he couldn't explain things, he repeated his words. "Lydia, I didn't do this. You have to believe me."

Lydia Cantrell, of the South Georgia we pioneers-settled-this-town-with-wagons-and-mules Cantrells, apparently wanted to believe him. She bobbed her head. "I do believe you. I do, Pastor Dev. But—"

He grabbed her by the hand, hauling her into the room as he shut the door. Which really threw him and her both, since he had never tried to touch her, not even so much as touch a strand of her hair or press his fingers along her arm as he opened a door for her. He'd always followed proper decorum when it came to his relationship with Lydia. But now, he had her by the arm, tugging her along with him as he grabbed equipment and weapons out of a steel briefcase. A briefcase he'd hoped never to use again.

Lydia looked at him in surprise. "What's with all those fancy gadgets?" When he didn't respond, she said, "You don't even carry a cell phone like most normal human beings."

It was true. He rarely bothered to use the computer they'd had installed two years ago at the church office. He mostly devoted his time to reading the Word, and taking care of members' needs and visitation. Dev was a stickler about visitation—always going out amongst his flock, sharing their good and bad times. Graduations—even from kindergarten—weddings, births, medical emergencies, cataract surgeries, deaths, anniversaries, christenings, baseball games, soccer matches, birthdays and retirements. You name it, Pastor Dev was there to celebrate it. The rest of the time, he worked on preaching the word of the Lord. And while he preached and tried to forget the past, Lydia sat in her same pew each and every Sunday, as devoted as ever. She was like a guiding light out in the congregation. A guiding light he refused to lose, ever. And now, she'd been exposed to the ugly side of his life. The secret life. This could get very messy, very fast.

As Lydia watched Pastor Dev gather strange little gadgets involving beepers and bullets, they heard a commotion at the hotel room door.

"Don't open it," he said, his fingers working at loading weapons and clicking against a slick cell phone. His whole expression had changed. He looked dangerous.

Lydia watched, awe and fear overcoming her. "What's going on?"

He grabbed her again. "Lydia, do you trust me?"

She didn't even have to think about that. "Of course, I do, Pastor Dev."

"Then you need to listen to me and follow my instructions, do you understand?"

She bobbed her head. "Yes. But—"

He hushed her with a finger to his lips. "No questions now. No time to explain. We have to get out of here."

"Excuse me?"

"I have to take you with me. They must be watching. They probably saw you come into the room. You're in danger."

"Oh, okay."

Lydia was completely baffled now. Why was she in danger and where was he taking her? And why on earth was Pastor Dev talking to her in that *Mission: Impossible* kind of voice, so intense and husky and brusque, so very different from his regular soft-spoken drawl?

"What's happening?" she managed to squeak out, even as they heard the banging on the door again. "Is this some sort of joke? I know how you and your buddies like to pull jokes on each other."

"No joke, Lydia," Pastor Dev said, guiding her to the adjoining room. And he now had a big gun in his hand. A sleek-looking gun with a long, thin barrel. It reminded her of something out of a spy movie. And she had no idea where it had been before. Probably inside that steel case he had hidden inside his real suitcase. Good thing they'd taken the bus to Atlanta. He never would have made it onto an airplane with all those gadgets or that gun.

Because Lydia stood frozen, staring at the gun, Dev shook her gently. "Lydia, I need you to be alert. Stay focused, okay?"

"Uh-huh."

"We have to get out of here."

"Uh-huh."

"Lydia, honey, are you with me?"

He moved close enough to see the solid fear in her pretty eyes. "Lydia?"

"I'm with you," she whispered, slowly moving her head again. "But I sure would like to know why we're getting out of here. I mean, we can't just leave your friend in the bathtub. We should call the police. We should—"

"No police," he said, his tone firm. "I'll explain everything later, I promise," he added in a soft whisper, his fingers brushing through her bangs.

She nodded and said, "Okay."

Then Dev reminded himself that she was probably in shock. Things had taken a distinctively different swing from the original plans. And getting Lydia involved in a life he'd tried to put behind him was definitely not in the plans. But he couldn't change that right now. He could only try to protect her.

"Let's go," he said, throwing a dark shirt toward her. "Put this on to camouflage yourself."

Lydia put on the shirt. "This smells like your laundry detergent," she said as he tugged at her sleeves. "I know which brand you use. I saw it on your To Do list one day. Not that I'd ever snoop."

Dev ignored her chatter. Let her chat. Lydia was a talker, especially when she got nervous. Right now, he had to focus; he had to get her out of here. "Button up," he ordered, keeping his tone firm.

She hurriedly buttoned the big shirt over her demur summer sweater, a dazed expression on her face.

"Ready?" he asked, his no-nonsense gaze focused on her as he looked directly into her hazel eyes. Dev wondered if she knew how much she meant to him. He'd have to tell her one day.

She nodded and held tight to her tote bag. "I think so."

Dev worked quickly to get them through the locked door to the empty room adjoining theirs. Putting a finger to his lips, he motioned for Lydia to stay quiet as he waited for the right moment. They managed to sneak down the hall just as the intruders came bursting into the other room.

"We're going to take the stairs down to the street," he explained, his voice back to normal now. Almost too normal. He stayed calm and in control, for Lydia's sake, but taking fourteen flights down to the street wasn't exactly a leisurely stroll. And leaving a room with his dead best friend in it wasn't too good, either. But he'd deal with that later. Much later.

"Okay," Lydia said. What else could she say, since she couldn't take her chances on the elevator and meet up with those Very Bad Guys? Her mama and daddy didn't raise a complete idiot, after all.

So down the stairs they went, flying so fast Lydia wondered if her sensible black Easy Spirit pumps were even touching the steps. But she was glad they were durable enough for someone on the run. She was amazed she didn't even get a blister. And she was also amazed that they didn't get shot. Lydia could hear the Very Bad Guys clunking down the stairs above them, the sound echoing like a death knell each time they rounded another floor. Then just as they reached the seventh floor, she felt the whiz and ping of a bullet ricocheting off the stair-well, very close to her head.

Screaming, Lydia put a hand up, as if that would

stop a bullet from killing her. The look in Pastor Dev's eyes told her the same thing. For once, the man looked scared. Scared for her, since he grabbed her and held her tight.

"Keep running, Lydia," Pastor Dev said to her, pushing her in front of him. Of course, he would be the gentleman, even in such a desperate life-or-death situation, so he naturally put himself in harm's way between her and the VBGs. That was a relief, until she started worrying that he'd get shot and then he'd be dead and she'd never grow old with him, or have his babies or be able to be the pastor's wife like she'd dreamed about for the last few years. Not to mention, the VBGs would still be after her. And she'd be all alone, wondering how she'd somehow wound up in Pastor Dev's hotel room with a dead body in the bathtub. Not to mention, having to explain all of that to the entire congregation.

But, she thought as she ran ahead of him, hadn't Pastor Dev asked her to trust him? Knowing that there was much more to this story, Lydia put her trust in God, praying to Him to help them out of this situation. Right now she only knew three things for sure. She was still in love with Pastor Dev, the Very Bad Guys were still chasing them and they were both in a whole lot of trouble.

TWO

So now they were on MARTA—the Metro Atlanta Rapid Transit System—heading north. Lydia was riding through the city on a commuter train at a very fast speed, sitting by a man she thought she knew. But she realized as she watched Pastor Dev jab at a sleek black PDA, that she didn't really know this man at all. Since when had he owned a BlackBerry, for goodness' sake? Her mama would laugh out loud at that notion.

Thinking of her mama and daddy back in Dixon, Lydia felt hot tears pricking at her eyes. She normally was a stand-up kind of girl, good in a pinch, solid in a crisis. But she had to admit, this was a bit much even for someone with her strong constitution. She didn't know what to do, so she clutched at her loaded tote bag, glad, at least, that she had her own supply of obsessive-compulsive ammunition tucked into the many pockets and packets inside. She had a cell phone—that might come in handy. She had Tylenol and Advil and a little bit of touch-up makeup. Okay, that was maybe a bit vain, but Lydia liked to look her best around Pastor Dev. Which meant she also had some of those travel toothpaste samples. And sample sizes of everything from deodorant to hair spray—all bought with her hard-earned money at the big discount store out on Highway 19 back in Dixon. And boy, had she earned her salary tonight, she thought, her feet hurting from all that pounding and running all over Atlanta.

And she also had a combination diary and day-book, which she was itching to record in right now. She'd always kept a diary, since she'd been old enough to form letters, as her mama liked to tell it. This mess tonight was gonna be a doozy of a story, she decided. But she wasn't at all sure how it was going to end.

By this time, it was very late and she was so tired she could barely hold her eyes open, so she missed the blur of skyscrapers that turned into suburbs as they headed out away from the city. She missed the ancient old oaks and the tall pines whizzing by. She didn't even notice the constant stream of traffic along Interstate 75. All she could see was her own shocked reflection in the dark window of the train. That and the image of Pastor Pierson's bloody body. She wanted to cry about that, but she couldn't find the tears. Yet. So she prayed for the dead minister, and for the evil person who had killed him.

Lydia had never felt so alone and frightened, even if Pastor Dev did seem like he could handle this situation.

Then it hit her—she could at least call her parents and let them know she was all right. She started digging in her tote, then proudly pulled out the little silver picture phone she'd bought at the big mall in Albany.

Dev watched her, knowing what he was about to do would only confuse her even more. He grabbed her hand, then gently took her phone away. "Don't do that, Lydia."

"I need to call my parents," she said, giving him a hurt look.

Dev figured she was wondering why he seemed so distant and businesslike. But he had to think; he had to figure a way to get her out of this mess.

Lydia's hurt soon changed into frustration. Just a tad irritated, she said, "Give me my phone back, please."

"Not just yet," he said, pulling out his own top-of-the-line, state-of-the-art, shiny black Treo. "We have to wait for further instructions."

Further instructions?

"Oh, okay." She gave him a wide-eyed look after he pocketed her plain little phone.

Dev hated to treat her this way, but if she called home, they could easily pinpoint the signal. "I know you think I'm crazy," he said, a twist of a smile playing at his lips, "but it's very important that you do not make contact with anyone. It's too dangerous, not just for you but for your family, too. Do you understand?"

"Too dangerous?" She stared over at him, her shock evident, her disbelief shimmering in her eyes. "Oh, okay," she said, not looking okay at all. "Honestly, you sound so condescending. I'm not some child about to have a tantrum." Before he could respond, she gave him a no-nonsense look. "You know what? I've had about enough of this game. You need to tell me what on earth is going on. Because I'm tired, I'm hungry and I'm getting mighty cranky. And that won't be good for either of us."

Now she had Dev's complete attention. Apparently, he wasn't the only one who could change from mild-mannered to dead serious in the blink of an eye. Thinking he'd better do something quick to calm her bad mood and make up for his rudeness, and because he didn't have time for theatrics, he gave her a long once-over look, then pulled her against him and said, "Rest."

"Huh?"

Not a very sophisticated response, Dev thought, but she had been fighting mad, so now she probably felt a bit off-kilter and befuddled by his quick mood change.

"Rest, Lydia," he said again, reaching around to tug her head against his shoulder. She felt like a small, fragile doll in his arms. "Just rest and then I'll explain everything. You don't deserve any of this, but you do deserve some answers."

"I sure do," she said into his T-shirt, causing him to become very much aware of her nearness. Then she mumbled, "Where'd you get this shirt, anyway?

You never wear T-shirts, except during basketball camp and volleyball games."

Dev decided he could at least talk about that, hoping it would make her forgive him for dragging her all over Atlanta. "My nephew, Scotty, gave it to me. To keep me safe."

Something about that confession must have tugged at Lydia's heart. Her next words were all husky with a little catch of emotion. "That is so sweet." Then she glanced up at him, her pretty angled face close to his. "I didn't even know you have a nephew."

"He's six." He felt the rumble of surprise moving through her. He didn't talk about Scotty much. "My sister's kid. They live up north. I don't get to see them much, but at least he's safe. Last time I visited, he was having an anxiety attack about starting first grade. I gave him a little pep talk and told him he was my hero. I knew he would be strong and courageous, for his mother's sake."

Dev heard her let out a sigh, then he held his breath as she snuggled deeper in his arms. He'd never realized how fresh her shampoo smelled—like apples and cinnamon.

"Now Scotty loves school. He told his mom I helped him to be strong. He wanted me to feel safe, too, so he sent me this shirt for my birthday. I promised him I'd always carry it with me whenever I travel. I just slipped it on tonight, because, well, because I miss him and I had him on my mind."

He wanted Lydia to understand that Scotty's

safety was important to him. Just as her safety was important to him, too. So maybe she could forgive him for being so brusque with her before. "I'm sorry, Lydia."

"For what?"

"For snapping at you. I have to protect you. I'm responsible for you."

"It's okay," she said, her words sounding sleepy. "That must be a very special shirt."

"It is. Scotty told me he said a prayer for me when he helped his mother wrap it."

"Now that just makes me want to cry," she whispered.

Dev prayed she didn't do that. But her voice sounded shaky. "I'm glad your shirt is so blessed." Then she wiggled closer and drifted off to sleep, the rattle and hum of the fast-moving train seeming to soothe her frazzled nerves.

Dev closed his eyes, too, then he kissed the top of her head while he held her there in his arms, against his blessed shirt.

Lydia woke with a start, trying to remember where she was. When she looked up to find Pastor Dev staring down at her, and looked down to find herself settled nicely into the crook of his strong arm, she gasped and sat straight up. "What—"

"The train's stopping. End of the line. We get off here," Pastor Dev explained. A little old lady across the aisle smiled over at them.

And as usual Lydia said, "Oh, okay." Until she remembered everything that had happened—dead body, bad guys, strange gadgets, a memory of a gentle kiss on her hair—she'd have to get back to that one. "Where are we?"

"Somewhere north of Atlanta," he replied as he tugged her to her feet. "Near Roswell, I believe." But he wasn't looking at her. Instead, he glanced all around, his dark eyes on full alert mode. But he was kind enough to let that little old blue-haired lady pass first. He checked the front of the passenger car, and the back, again and again. He gave other passengers a hard, daring stare which seemed to make all of them quake in their boots. Except the grandma. She simply smiled her sweet, wrinkled smile and held on to her sensible black purse as she slowly ambled her way toward the train doors.

Pastor Dev did one more search. "I think we're safe. Let's go."

So they got off MARTA along with a few other people—probably night workers coming home from the city. It was very late, actually early morning, the wee hours, as Lydia's mama would say. She'd never stayed out this late in her life, even in all her sorority days at UGA. But then, she reminded herself, things on this night were not at all what they seemed.

And neither was the man pulling her away from the cluster of passengers heading to their parked cars or waiting rides. She worried about the old woman. Did she have a ride home? Was she all alone in the world?

But Pastor Dev didn't give Lydia time to visit

with the old woman. Lydia watched as the spry woman shuffled off in another direction.

"What now?" she asked, breathless from being tugged at a fast-footed pace across the cracked commuter parking lot.

Pastor Dev stopped underneath a large oak tree. As if right on cue, his fancy phone beeped. "Yes?" he said into the phone. Then he said something really odd. "Have we put out a search for any lost sheep?"

She had to blink at that one. But she'd figured out not to ask questions, not when he was in that instruction mode, anyway. So she just listened. That's how she'd learned so much in school. She was a good listener.

"Copy," he said into the phone. Then "Where is the way to the dwelling of light?"

If Lydia hadn't known better, she would have thought he was quoting scripture. Job, if she remembered correctly. She had always been good at memorizing Bible passages back in Sunday school.

But then he said, "Yes, I understand." And that was that.

"We have to go," he told her after he put the tiny phone away. "I have to get you to a safe place."

She looked around. The train was gone. The carpoolers and night shift workers were gone. They were all alone at a train station somewhere in North Georgia. She glanced around, seeing the lights of the city miles away. "How are we going to get out of here?"

"We walk," he said, as if this was the most normal

thing in the world. Then he kept right on talking in that calm, normal voice. "It's not seemly—you and I running off together. I have to consider your reputation. I need to get you to a safe house where there are highly trained chaperones who can help me watch over you. Before I leave."

That got her dander up. "What did you say?" she asked, stopping and digging her heels into the asphalt. It still felt warm from the spring day. Or maybe that heat was coming from the steam rising inside of her.

He turned, let out a sigh. "Lydia, you shouldn't be here. I would never forgive myself if something happened to you."

And because that kind of sounded as if he cared about her just a tiny bit, she cut him some slack. But she still needed answers. "Nothing will happen to me if you'll just tell me the truth."

He stood there, his eyes touching on her face before he glanced off into the darkness. "We need to find a vehicle."

"No, you need to tell me the truth." She skipped two beats, giving him ample time to chime right in, then she let him have it good and proper. "Look, Pastor Dev, I've known you for close to three years now and…well, never in those three years have you ever so much as raised your voice at me. But tonight, tonight, something changed. I mean, besides the dead man in your bathtub and that big, scary gun, and those goons chasing us. *You* changed right in front of my eyes. And I do believe that means you owe me some kind of explanation." Then she took off, her pumps pounding pavement. "You can talk while we walk."

He caught up with her right away, reaching for her swinging arm. "Okay, all right. But the less you know, the safer you'll be."

"I can't be safe if I don't know what I'm fighting."

He considered that for a minute. "You're right. And you're a very smart woman."

"Well, at least you've noticed that about me."

That comment made him frown in that kind of confused way men do when they don't understand the underlying meaning. But she let it slide. As much as she'd like to have had a real heart-to-heart with the man, what she needed more was concrete information.

"Go on," she said, coaxing him like a teacher coaxing a kindergartner.

"You're right about me. I'm not what I seem."

"I got that right after you pulled out that big gun," she snapped back. "Not to mention the dead man."

He frowned again, a new respect for her in his eyes. "Before I came to Dixon, I was...something besides a preacher."

"Uh-huh. What?"

He let out a breath. "After I got out of seminary school, I was approached by a very elite organization and asked if I'd like to join their ranks." He shrugged. "I fit the profile exactly. Athletic, excellent grades, exemplary conduct. Single and young. And very devoted to the Lord."

"You do fit all those qualifications," she blurted

out. Then she put a hand over her big mouth. "Keep talking."

He gave her another strange look, but continued. "This organization is so top secret, that I couldn't even tell my immediate family what I would be doing. I had to use a cover."

"A cover?" Lydia shot a glance over at him. He looked completely sincere. "You mean, like a spy?"

"Yes, something like that. But more like a Christian operative."

"A Christian operative?"

"Yes. I'm like a soldier, only I don't work for the government. I work for the church."

"You're a soldier? For the church?"

She knew she sounded stupid, but Pastor Dev didn't look at her as if she were stupid. Instead, he looked at her as if he were hoping she'd understand. Which she didn't.

"I know it sounds like something out of a science fiction novel, but I'm telling you the truth. And before I go any further, you have to promise you will not divulge anything I'm telling you. It could mean your life."

She stopped on the side of the road. "Well, when you put it that way—"

He whirled her around so fast, she felt as though she was back on that train. "I'm serious, Lydia. This is not a game. We are in a very dangerous situation."

The way he looked at her gave her hope, even while his words scared her silly. He looked as though he really cared about her. "Okay," she said in a tiny voice. "I'm sorry."

Then he touched a hand to her hair, sending nice little shivers down her backbone. "No, I'm the one who's sorry. I shouldn't have gotten you involved in this."

"I'm here now," she said, her practical nature taking over. "Might as well spill the rest, so I can be prepared."

He smiled then. "That's what I like about you. You are so organized and sensible."

Wow, that kind of remark could sure go to a girl's head, right? Now Lydia was even more anxious to find out what he'd gotten her involved in. "Just tell me, Pastor Dev. So I can help you."

He stood back, then started walking again, his eyes ever alert to the shadows along the highway and the forest noises off along the fence line. "For ten years now, I've belonged to an organization called CHAIM. That's Hebrew for 'life.'"

"Nice," she said, suddenly caught up in what he was saying. "What does this organization do, exactly?"

He stopped again, and put his arms on hers. "We save people."

Lydia's heart thumped against her rib cage. "As in?"

"This is the secretive part, Lydia. My parents thought I was off doing missionary work, but I wasn't—at least not in the usual way. CHAIM stands for Christians for Amnesty, Intervention and Ministry. We go into other countries and rescue Christians who are in danger."

Lydia let that soak in, then put a hand to her mouth. "You mean, you're some sort of special ops agent?"

He nodded. "Yes, I was for seven years before I came to Dixon. I had to retire from the force. We've saved hostages, we've helped stranded Christian missionaries out of volatile situations, and we've rescued good, honest people who've found them-selves in the wrong place at the wrong time. Because we don't work for the government, we have our own set of rules. We try not to do any harm—we just get in, get out, and save lives on both sides."

"So you're not violent and mercenary?"

He looked away, a darkness settling in his eyes. "Only if we have to defend ourselves or the people we're helping."

That thump in her heart was at full throttle now. "How? Why? I don't understand."

"I know it's hard, seeing me in such a different way. But you're safe as long as you're with me. You have my word on that."

"But if you're retired—"

He glanced around. "Someone wants me perma-nently retired. Whoever killed Charles Pierson ob-viously thought they had me."

Lydia's heart sputtered. She couldn't breath. Hadn't she figured this out already, since she'd been chased and shot at? But hearing him say it out loud made it so real. "You mean, you might have been the one—"

His voice went low. "I gave Charles a key to my room, and told him to meet me there. I had to talk to another colleague before our meeting to discuss my speech. Charles went up ahead of me. They must have ambushed him. It should have been me."

She stared up at him, flabbergasted at what he was telling her. "You could have been killed tonight?"

He nodded. "Yes. I'm out of CHAIM and no one, not even the other operatives, knows where I've been assigned. But someone has breached the security of the entire organization. Just to have me killed. And I'm pretty sure I know who that someone is."

Lydia's whole body was shaking now. She couldn't breathe, she couldn't think beyond the fact that Pastor Dev might have been killed tonight. Up until now, she'd wanted to believe it had all been some sort of mistake, that they weren't the target. She looked back up at him, tears brimming in her eyes. And then she started shaking so badly, she felt sick to her stomach. With a rush, everything that had happened came at her, causing her to grow weak. "You could have been killed."

He touched his thumb to her chin. "I might still be killed, Lydia. And you right along with me, if they find us. That's what I've been trying to tell you."

He caught her in his arms just before she passed out.

THREE

Dev hated to bring Lydia out of the relative peace of her little fainting spell. But he had to, so he carried her to a big stone bench. "Lydia, wake up." He held her in his arms, scoping the spot just as the little old lady they'd seen on the train came charging around the corner.

Obviously trying to focus, Lydia lifted her head and spotted the woman. And in her usual Lydia way, said, "How nice. She's worried about us." While Dev went into combat mode, Lydia sent the woman a reassuring smile. Then asked, "How long has that nice little lady been tailing us, anyway?"

"She's not so very nice, and she really isn't a lady at all," Dev whispered. There she stood, glaring at Lydia and Dev through her bifocals. And she was packing more than just antacid and Advil.

Even in her stupor of confusion, Lydia seemed to figure things out. "That woman's gun is much bigger than yours, Pastor Dev."

"You can say that again."

The woman aimed the gun right at Lydia and Dev. Then she spoke. "'Will your riches, or all the mighty forces, keep you from distress?'"

"Job again," Lydia murmured, her shock obviously bone deep. And it was about to get worse, Dev thought.

Everything after that was in fast-forward. Dev pushed Lydia down into the leaves and grass behind the bench, his hand on her back. "Stay down," he hissed.

Since Lydia seemed paralyzed with fear, staying down wasn't a problem. She cringed low as Dev managed to position himself behind the concrete back of the bench, trying to protect her with his body. But her head came up in spite of his best effort as she strained to peek at their assailant.

Then she gasped. Probably because she saw what Dev had already figured out. The old lady wasn't actually a woman. She was a *he*. A wiry young man dressed like an old lady. And that man was trying to kill them. Shots clinked and pinged all around them, but Dev didn't let that bother him. He kept Lydia's head down, his body protecting hers, and kept himself out of the line of fire. While he waited for his chance.

Amazed and paralyzed with fear, Lydia watched him—but it was like a slow-motion dance of some sort, surreal and bizarre. He stood, then crouched forward, all the while firing that big-barreled gun at the enemy. One of the shots hit its mark. But Pastor

Dev didn't kill the VEP—the Very Bad Guys had been elevated in Lydia's mind to Very Evil People. Pastor Dev shot the man in the leg, causing him to drop his weapon and roll around in agony. The wound must have hurt something awful from the way the man was screaming.

"Don't worry, I just maimed him," Pastor Dev explained, in a tone he might use to say, "Don't you just love long walks in the woods, Lydia?"

"What if he tells someone about us?" Lydia asked as Pastor Dev sank back behind the bench.

"He won't. Because then he'd have to explain his presence here. And he was never here. Neither were we."

"Part of the cover?"

"Yes."

Lydia put her hands over her head and closed her eyes, thinking of her nice little garage apartment back in Dixon. She loved that tiny apartment. It sat right over an old train depot that had been converted into a thriving antiques and collectibles minimall, complete with a country diner, both run by Lydia's Aunt Mabel. She thought of the wonderful view of downtown Dixon—which encompassed about one square block. She thought of the great old live oak right outside her window, and the Carnegie Library and the Dixon Pharmacy and Soda Shoppe, safe, secure places with ready supplies of books, ice cream, hair spray and flavored lattes. What more could a girl ask for?

Right then, Lydia could have used a white chocolate mocha latte. She wanted so badly to be back in her four-poster bed with the frilly magnolia-embossed comforter and sheets, reading a good novel from the library, her beloved portrait of Clark Gable and Vivian Leigh in *Gone With The Wind* hanging on the long wall opposite her bed. Her cat Rhett would be curled up beside her on the bed, his one black patched eye contrasting sharply with his white face. Oh, how she wished to hold Rhett.

"Lydia, are you all right?"

She heard Pastor Dev's words echoing across her mind, tugging her away from that peaceful, normal scene and back to the dark, scary not-so-normal woods. "I'm just dandy. Where's that strange old woman?"

"She—he's over there in the bushes, moaning."

"Should we help him?"

"No. He won't die. He's trained to stop the bleeding."

"That sure makes me feel better. What now? Will he try to follow us?"

"No. He's injured. He'll have to report back to his superiors that his mission has failed."

"And just who does he work for? Surely not CHAIM?"

"That's the question, isn't it? And that's what our mission is all about. We have to find out who's behind this and who sent him."

"Do you have an idea?"

"I have a theory. But I have to get to a secure place before I can figure this out."

They heard more moans, but Lydia didn't feel as much empathy now for the old woman–possible killer.

"Not my problem," she said, getting up to brush off her clothes. "Let's get out of here."

"Good idea." Pastor Dev looked around, probably thinking there were others lurking in the shadows. Or maybe Lydia was the only one thinking about that possibility.

"We'll cut through the woods until we reach the river," Pastor Dev whispered. "Then we'll find a way to get to our next destination."

Lydia didn't even know they were near a river, but a few miles later, sure enough she could hear a soft gurgling off in the distance. The Chattahoochee? Or maybe all that gurgling was coming from the bleeding man in the granny wig who was probably hobbling along after them.

"What will be our next destination?" she asked, afraid to hear the answer.

"New Orleans," Pastor Dev said as he shoved her into the shadowy oaks and pines.

She gave him just enough time to get them hidden, then stopped. "I can't go to New Orleans. My parents would have a royal hissy fit about that."

"I'll be with you," Pastor Dev said in that condescending, I-know-best voice. "You'll be safe."

"Not in that city. My grandmother says the French Quarter's a regular den of iniquity."

Taking her by the hand, he stalked through the woods as if he knew exactly where he was going.

"Not all of New Orleans is like that, Lydia, and besides, you don't have any choice. Those are my instructions."

"To get us to New Orleans?"

"Yes. We need to get out of Georgia."

"Is the dwelling of light there—in New Orleans?"

He shook his head, then let out a sigh. "You are so smart."

She refused to let flattery stop her. "Just answer me."

"Yes—that's a code for a safe house. Can you trust me?"

"You said I don't have any choice."

He gave her a long, steady look. One of his commando looks. "I'm sorry about that. Do you trust me?"

"I'm trying, Pastor Dev. But you have to admit this is all a bit new for me. You might need to give me a few minutes to adjust."

"Okay. Take all the time you need. But remember, you have to listen to me and trust my decisions."

"Okay."

They walked along in silence for a few minutes. Lydia used the time to pout. She liked to be in control of any and all situations and right now she felt completely out of control. "Can I at least call my parents now?"

"They have been apprised of the situation."

Lydia stopped again, then glanced over at him. "They have? Who did the apprising?"

"We have operatives everywhere. The situation

has been explained in detail. Your parents know you're safe and with me."

"Somehow, that doesn't make me feel any better."

In a lightning move, he tugged her close. Which, in spite of her pouting, did make her feel better. "You shouldn't be here, Lydia," he said, his gaze moving over her face.

That soft-spoken, regret-filled statement didn't set well with Lydia, since she had always dreamed of being in his arms. But she understood what he meant. Actually, neither of them should be here— technically speaking.

Lydia shrugged. "I'm here now. No use crying over spilled milk."

Then he started laughing. That didn't help Lydia's mood. She backed away from him, pushing her hands through her tangled hair. "You think that's funny?"

"Yes. I mean, no." He pulled her back into his arms.

"It's just that…Lydia, you amaze me. You are so practical and pragmatic. *Spilled milk.*"

"Well, this is a big old puddle of a mess, don't you agree?"

He probably could tell she was getting all worked up. He didn't try to hug her again. Instead, he stopped laughing and let out a sigh. "That is correct. A big mess that I've somehow managed to get a nice girl like you involved in. Not only that, but one of the best men I know died tonight. Because of me."

What could she say to that? She'd been so scared

and confused, she hadn't even stopped to think about his friend. She couldn't resort to bickering and sarcasm after hearing the anguish in his words. Especially his next statement.

"This is all my fault."

Since Pastor Dev walked on ahead, she had to follow him or risk getting left out in the Georgia woods with all the varmints and bugs and men in wigs. She caught up with him, but remained silent, sending up prayers for the soul of his friend. Lydia's mother had always told her silence was golden. Since the woods were so dark and quiet, with only the moonlight and stars to guide them, she decided it was a good time to go to God in prayer about this whole bizarre situation.

Lydia worried as she prayed, not only about herself and her life, but also about Pastor Dev. He was right. He'd lost one of his best friends back in that hotel room. Now she reckoned he was grieving in a kind of delayed reaction way. And what about Reverend Pierson's family? How was anyone going to explain this to them? What about the authorities back in Atlanta? Would they be hushed up, or would Lydia's and Pastor Dev's names and pictures be plastered all over the news? How would they ever get out of this?

She asked God all of these questions as they walked along, then she asked Him to show them the way. Lydia knew in her heart that Pastor Dev had to be telling her the truth, but she wondered how in the world such a good and decent man had become involved with killers and thugs. Then she reminded herself CHAIM was supposedly a Christian organization, meant to help those in need. And that would mean sometimes having to deal with dangerous, unscrupulous people.

He's one of the good guys, Lydia, she reminded herself as she chanced a glance over at him. *Remember that.* Then she tried to imagine all the places he'd been, the horrible things he'd seen in his operative days. And he'd said he had to retire? What did that mean? Not, *I retired,* but *I had to retire.* There was a big difference in that particular wording. And just who wanted him dead?

He'd said he thought he knew who.

So she asked him. "Who's behind this?"

"I can't tell you."

"But you think you know, right?"

"I'm pretty sure, yes."

"Did you do something bad, for someone to want you dead?"

Dev didn't speak for a while. Their feet crunched on leaves and twigs, each sound causing Lydia to walk closer to him. He grabbed her hand to keep her from tripping against his feet, since she was like a shadow right at his heels.

"I didn't do anything bad," he finally said. "I did do something that made some people very angry at me. But I had my reasons."

"Such as?"

"I can't explain it right now, Lydia. I've got people

investigating things. It's very complicated." That was an understatement. He didn't know where to begin.

"Yeah, well, it would have been nice to be forewarned about…your past life. I've known you for a while now, and I never would have guessed—"

"That's how CHAIM wants things. We're trained to fit right in, wherever we go. Sometimes, we fit in too well."

"You can say that again. Are you even a real preacher?"

He looked over at her, masking the piercing hurt her doubt brought. "Of course I am. I attended seminary in New Orleans. I trained to be a minister. I just got sidetracked for a while." Then he shook his head. "No, that's not exactly correct. Being in CHAIM taught me more about being a Christian than anything else, even preaching."

"I guess so, what with all the deception and intrigue. I'm sure that comes in handy each Sunday when you're quoting the Gospels to all the good, decent folks back in Dixon."

"I know you're confused and angry," he said, taking her hand again. "But my experiences in CHAIM have helped me with my messages each Sunday. My past life has taught me compassion, and understanding and unconditional love." Then he squeezed her hand tight. "Lydia, I can't bear you being angry at me. But I certainly don't blame you." He let out a long sigh, his hands dropping to his side. This wasn't going to be easy, not with Lydia. She was too innocent for this. "If I've lost *your* respect, then I truly am lost."

* * *

That comment shut her up, good and proper. But she glowed in her silence, and she didn't exactly feel like pouting anymore. He wanted her respect above all else? Did that even hint at any type of feelings he might have for her, other than those of friend and coworker and fellow Christian?

Lydia swallowed hard, prayed for guidance, then said, "You *did* have my respect, and you still do. I just wish I'd had your trust so you could have told me about all of this."

He pushed a hand over his face. "It's not a matter of trust. CHAIM doesn't allow us to give out information. We tell no one. We don't share the details of our jobs. That would put too many people in danger. And I think someone has done exactly that—given our identities and our locations away. There are people all over the world who'd like to see all of the CHAIM operatives dead."

"Starting with you?"

"It looks that way, yes."

"But now that I know about CHAIM, can't you give me a few more hints? I need to be prepared for the worst."

He heaved them both up an embankment, then stopped to take in the lay of the land while Lydia stopped to marvel at his strength—not just his outer physical strength, but an inner core that now radiated around him and made him seem powerful and heroic in her eyes. And made her wonder, yet again, just how many secrets he was carrying.

Too tired to figure all that out, Lydia concentrated on their surroundings. The woods were shrouded in a blanket of gray moonlight, the river glistened like a silver necklace. She could hear the rustling of forest creatures off in the distance. At least, she hoped it was forest creatures and not humans dressed in disguise, coming for them.

Since he just stood there like a good-looking block of stone, she reminded Pastor Dev again. "I need to understand. I like details, I like to be organized and prepared. So I need to know everything, just in case."

He got moving then, his boots stomping through the underbrush. "No, you don't. You just need to do exactly as I say, for your own protection and safety."

She hurried to catch him, then stopped to stare at his retreating back. "Will you ever tell me all of it? I mean, why we're really being chased and what you did to cause this?"

"Probably not. You're better off not knowing."

And that's the only answer she got. He refused to give her the details—for her own protection, of course. Lydia was getting mighty tired of being kept in the dark for her own protection. But then, what choice did she have? Right now, she could only follow the man she loved as they marched blindly along.

So she stomped after him in her sensible pumps, so very glad that he at least thought she was amazing, practical and pragmatic. The compliments couldn't get much better. The man might be able to leap tall buildings in a single bound, but he didn't have a clue as to a woman's heart. Not one clue.

Lydia didn't know where she was going to wind up after this. Right now, she just had to find a way to survive New Orleans. If they ever got there. But after what happened when they did get there, Lydia would have rather stayed hidden in the woods of North Georgia.

FOUR

"Why New Orleans?" Lydia asked an hour later as they drove over the Alabama state line, heading for Mississippi and eventually, Louisiana.

Pastor Dev shifted the gears of the beat-up Chevy truck he'd managed to "buy" off a kid near Marietta, his eyes straight ahead on the back road they were taking to the Interstate. Lydia didn't try to figure out how he'd arranged to buy the truck, but then, finagling a truck from a teenager in the middle of the night was only one of his many talents, she imagined.

"I told you, there's a safe house there. It's the least likely place anyone would look for us."

"Now that makes sense," she replied, tilting her head back on the rough fabric of the seat. Then she glanced over at him again. "Are you sure about my parents? I don't want them to worry."

"They know you're safe."

He wasn't much for giving out unnecessary information. And now that Lydia thought about it, he'd always been that way. Not a big talker—about himself. But he could talk a bobcat through a pack of bulldogs, faithwise. Was that the mark of a good minister? Or the cover of a man full of secrets?

Tired of all the questions running amok inside her head, she decided to try a different tack. "What happens in New Orleans? I mean, do we just sit and wait?"

He shook his head. "No, you rest and I work."

"Work? What kind of work?"

"I have to locate my superiors, let them know I'm okay. I'll need to give a thorough report, then wait for further instructions."

Lydia was getting mighty tired of this "further instructions" business. She didn't like being undercover, not one little bit. But she didn't want to ruffle Commando Dev's already riled feathers, so she tried to sound excited. "That should be interesting." Then she closed her eyes. "What about Pastor Pierson?"

He didn't speak for a full minute. Lydia slanted her eyes to watch him for signs of wear and tear. "Are you okay?"

Pastor Dev tapped the steering wheel in a soft gentle cadence, then glanced at the NASCAR-emblazoned key chain that dangled like a necklace around the truck's rearview mirror. "Arrangements are being made. The official report—a break-in and robbery."

"What about us? What's the official report on us?"

"We were in a different room. We were never there."

"They switched your room?"

"Yes. To protect you. And to keep my cover. The official report will be that we had to leave the conference suddenly. After a few days, the official report will be that we're on a working retreat."

Lydia felt her dander rising, but she held back. "Y'all like to stretch the truth to the limits with all this undercover stuff, don't you?"

"It's for our safety and protection."

"Yeah, there is that."

He didn't answer, and Lydia felt small and petty for being so snippy. But then, it was late and she was tired and still suffering from shell shock. And since she hadn't been through the school of special ops etiquette, she thought she was doing a fairly good job of winging it.

"So Pastor Pierson's family thinks he was attacked and robbed? And that's it?"

"That has to be it. And that is the truth. He was attacked."

But Lydia could tell by the way he stated the obvious, that wasn't all of it. One of his best friends was dead, and she could see the weight of that pulling at Pastor Dev's strong shoulders. "I'm sorry about your friend."

"Me, too. Get some rest, Lydia. We have a long way to go."

Then he went completely blank, effectively shutting her out. Lydia felt the burn of tears in her eyes, but she stubbornly refused to give in to the need to cry herself a little river. So she prayed, her eyes closed, her mind emptying of all the questions and the unpleasant images. She put an image of the Lord front and center in her head and held to that image as she asked Him to protect them. And while she prayed, she wondered if might made right. If the need for the better good of all made up for the small sins of omission. If the end justified the means. Was this all in the name of God? Or was this man's way of misinterpreting God's word?

Either way, Lydia was in the thick of it now. There was no turning back. She needed her faith now more than ever. And so did Pastor Dev.

Dev exited off the Interstate at a little roadside rest area just past Montgomery, making sure they were in a secluded, hidden spot. Glancing over at Lydia, he was relieved to see that she was sleeping, her head pressed against the window, her hands crossed in her lap. Good. She needed her rest. The poor woman had never been through anything like this night, he was sure. He knew this simply because he knew Lydia. She was a good girl. Everyone loved Lydia. *Everyone.*

Dev opened his door and deftly hopped out of the souped-up truck, careful not to wake Lydia. He needed to breathe. He needed to think. He needed to pray.

So he went to an old stone picnic table, which sat in clear view of the truck, his mind alert to the sounds from both the highway and the hills behind them. He'd forgotten how tense this work could make a man. He'd forgotten how complacent he'd become, living in Dixon, preaching God's word. But he hadn't forgotten all the years of being in CHAIM. How could a man ever forget that?

God's word? *What is that now?* he wondered as he placed his head in his hands and tried to gather his thoughts.

Someone had breached a very tight-knit security. Someone had taken a mighty big risk.

"Do you want me dead so much?"

Had he said that out loud? Dev looked around at the moonlit little roadside park, a discarded soda bottle winking at him in the dark while he wished his former friend and colleague could answer that question for him. So much water underneath the bridge; so much pain held captive in his friend's lonely heart. "Are you the one, Eli?"

To keep his mind sane, Dev once again checked his Treo. No messages. He half expected to find one from his rogue associate, telling him exactly where the next hit would be—just because Eli was that kind of guy—precise and brilliant and apparently past the breaking point. But there was nothing. No messages from his superiors, or his wayward friend or from the Lord, either. So he sat in the dark and pondered and prayed as he thought of dear, sweet Lydia, so trusting, so innocent, so…Lydia. He went over everything inside his head, wondering if he still had it in him to do this kind of work. He was rusty, softened by the kind folks of Dixon, softened by the kind eyes of the woman sleeping in the truck. He'd actually believed it was all over and behind him, all this secretiveness and espionage, all this creeping into darkness. He'd hoped—

He glanced back at the truck and thought of Lydia. What must she think of him now? What happened to his hopes and dreams now?

He felt completely hopeless, completely alone in the dark. He wanted to cry out, he wanted to revolt, to run. But he couldn't do any of those things. So he just sat there, staring at the truck, his mind centered on the woman inside. As he sat, he relived the horrible moment he'd found his hotel room door open and saw his friend's body slumped over in the bathtub. And somehow, he'd known that his safe, blessed life in Dixon was about to change. If only he'd had time to warn Lydia, to save her from all of this.

He'd never forget the look on her face when she'd walked into that room. Her fear and revulsion still shocked Dev to his core. How he wanted to protect her, to keep her safe. But what if he failed?

Dev did what he'd always done in tough situations. He turned to God. "'With my whole heart have I sought thee,'" he quoted from Psalms. "'O let me not wander from thy commandments.'"

And then he wept.

Lydia thought she heard weeping. Coming awake with a gasp, she followed that with a groan. Her neck felt as if someone had twisted it into a French braid and her head didn't feel much better. It pounded and tightened as if someone were truly pulling her hair and twisting it without mercy. She couldn't remember where she was. Then, as memory pushed through her disorientation, fear replaced all of those concerns.

She was alone in the truck.

"Pastor Dev?" she croaked, her eyes adjusting to the still, dark countryside. She sat straight up, pushing at her hair, her gaze moving over the moon-dappled woods. A tattered white plastic grocery bag hung like a flag of surrender off a moss-draped live oak, and the moon lounged with a smirk right up there in the night sky. An unfamiliar fear gripped Lydia, making her take in several rushed breaths. She wanted away from this place. But where was Pastor Dev?

And then she saw him.

He was sitting on a picnic table a few feet from the truck, a dark, somber silhouette with his head in his hands. At first, he looked so still and unmoving, Lydia thought she was just imagining him there. But then, she saw the slight shaking of his shoulders and heard the intake of a long, shuddering sob.

Lydia's fear dissipated like a cloud parting for the moon. Her heart lurched as she went into overdrive, opening the truck door to make a straight run toward him, her pumps echoing across the asphalt with a clip-clop cadence.

"Pastor Dev?" she said, not stopping to think of her actions as she grabbed his hands. They were wet with tears.

He looked up at her, his eyes dark with torment

before they became fully alert and clear. Then he tried to push her away. "No."

"Yes," Lydia said, determination and love bringing out her fiercely protective instincts. She might not be highly trained in undercover maneuvers, but she was extremely skilled in the compassion department. "Yes." She pulled him into her arms, her whispers filled with her own tears. "Let me help you. Lean on me. Let me help you, please."

He stared at her long and hard, an armor of pain and confusion shining in his eyes, then he pulled her into his arms and held her while he cried, rocking back and forth against her, his head on her shoulder, his big hands clutching at her back, until her shirt was as wet as his own.

Lydia cried, too, because it tore her heart apart to see this strong, solid man in such bad shape. She knew he was just having a delayed reaction to seeing his friend murdered, and to whatever forces had pulled him back into that other life. What man could handle that? Not even one as strong and sure as this one, Lydia thought, as she held him and stroked a hand through his hair. "I'm so sorry," she whispered. "So sorry."

He pulled away to look up at her, his eyes so soft and misty and full of a dark longing, Lydia wondered if she *were* dreaming. For a single heartbeat of a second, she thought he might kiss her. But instead, he pushed at her, then jumped away from the table as if the solid stone was on fire.

"We need to get back on the road," he said, wiping his eyes with a swat of his hand.

"Okay."

Lydia's heart fell apart with a shattering like little fractured bits of stained glass falling from a window. She stared after him, then she followed him back to the dark truck. She wanted to wake up safe in Dixon. She wanted to get up and drink her two cups of coffee and get dressed and walk down the street to the church, where she'd find various volunteers waiting to help her with her duties there. And she wanted to find Pastor Dev sitting at his desk eating a banana muffin from Aunt Mabel's diner. He would offer her a bite. She would decline, but she'd bring him an extra cup of coffee to wash it down. She *wanted* that so much.

She wanted normal back.

And she wanted Pastor Dev back.

They drove over Lake Pontchartrain as the sun was rising behind them. A fine mist of fog rose off the lake, rays of newborn sky filtering through to wash the dawn in bright white-pink light.

"We'll be safe here," Pastor Dev said, his voice weak and hoarse from not speaking. Not since his meltdown at the roadside park, at least.

Lydia had honored his need to remain silent. She had some thinking of her own to do. Now she could tell he was trying to reassure her.

"I'm a burden to you, aren't I?" she asked now. "You're stuck with me—with protecting me."

His smile was rusty. "I don't mind that burden."

Something inside Lydia deepened and widened at

that simple statement. He was that kind of man. He'd gladly carry the burdens of those he loved.

Does he love me? she wondered now, wishing, hoping and praying. Then she told herself to shut up. *Don't be selfish. Please get us out of this, Lord. Keep him safe.* That would be enough for a lifetime, Lydia decided.

"I'm sorry you have to watch out for me."

He looked over at her as they came across the Mississippi River into New Orleans. "Don't apologize, Lydia. None of this is your fault."

"It's not yours, either," she replied, watching for signs of distress.

But he was back to being Commando Dev now, all business with brusque, curt replies. "Yes, it is. But I don't have time to explain that right now. I need to brief you."

Brief her? Lydia accepted that things were probably about to get dicey again. "Go ahead."

"The safe house—it won't be all white picket fences and magnolias in a garden."

She let that soak in, her mind reeling with images of dark, smoke-filled alleyways and double-locked doors. "Keep talking."

"It's called Kissie's Korner. It's in the Quarter."

"My mama—"

"Would want you safe," he finished before she could voice her mother's disapproval.

"Not in a place like that. It sounds so—"

"Decadent?" he asked with that tight little smile. She didn't dare look at him. "Yes."

"It's a blues club. Some of the best blues and jazz musicians in the world have passed through Kissie's place. But that's just a cover."

"Uh-huh. So you're telling me that even though this place sounds like the devil's playground, it's really as squeaky clean as a church pew?"

He actually chuckled. "Ah, Lydia, I'm almost glad you're with me on this."

That caused her heart to glow just like the dawn all around them, bright and full of hope. "Thanks, I think," she said to hide that glow. She had to keep reminding herself she did not want to be here. "But you didn't answer my question."

"Kissie's Korner is a very clean place, faithwise. Kissie takes in troubled teens, turns them toward the Lord and sets them on their way. She's probably saved more teens in her thirty-five years of being an operative than anyone else on the planet."

"That is mighty respectable."

"Kissie is a good-hearted woman. She loves the Lord and serves only Him. She doesn't put up with any bunk, I can tell you."

"Drunken, rowdy blues players constitute bunk in my book."

"Kissie doesn't allow for any of that kind of stuff. Her place is a coffee bar."

Lydia's mouth fell open. "Nothing stronger than caffeine? I don't get it."

"Neither do the ones who try to pull anything. She boots them out, but they usually come back, begging for redemption. Kissie is that good."

"Wow."

"Wow is right," he said as he steered the truck down a narrow street just on the fringes of the French Quarter near Louis Armstrong Park. Then he parked and glanced around, his eyes doing a recon roll. "We're here."

Lydia looked up at the massive house in front of them, a soft gasp of shock shuddering through her body. It looked so old and dilapidated she had to wonder if it had been here since the beginning of time, or at least since the beginning of New Orleans. Two-storied and painted a sweet baby-blue, the house leaned so far to the left, a lush hot-pink bougainvillea vine actually floated out and away from it. The house reminded Lydia of an old woman holding a lacy handkerchief. The tall, narrow windows were surrounded with ancient gray-painted hurricane shutters. Antique wrought-iron tables and chairs filled the lacy balconies and porches. Petunias in various clay pots bloomed with wild abandonment all around the tottering, listing porch, while a magenta-colored hibiscus flared out like a belle's skirt right by the steps. And a white-lettered sign over the front porch stated Kissie's in curled, spiraling letters that matched the curling, spiraling mood of the house.

"This is a safe house?"

"Completely safe." Pastor Dev came around the truck to help Lydia out. "Trust me."

"Trust you?"

"You will, won't you, Lydia?"

The way he looked at her, the way he asked that one simple question, made Lydia feel as sideways and unstable as this old house, while the look in his eyes made her want to stand tall and believe in him with all her heart.

"I guess I have to, now, don't I?"

His smile was as brittle as the peeling paint on the house. "Yes, I'm afraid you do. Because, I have to warn you, this is only the beginning."

"Oh, great," Lydia said, using humor to hide her apprehension. "You mean, there's more ahead?"

"Lots more before it's over," he said. "They won't stop until they find us."

And this time, he wasn't smiling.

FIVE

"Get yourself on in here, man, and give Kissie a good and proper hug."

The tall, big-boned woman stood at the door of the leaning house, the colorful beads on her long dreadlocks bouncing against her ample arms and shoulders. She wore a brightly patterned silk caftan that swished each time she chuckled and smiled. And she smelled like vanilla and spice.

That was Lydia's first impression of Kissie Pierre, code name, Woman at the Well. Lydia watched as the voluptuous Kissie grabbed Pastor Dev and hugged him so tightly, he nearly lost his breath. But he didn't seem to mind. He returned Kissie's exuberant hug with one of his own, a gentle smile on his face as he winked at Lydia over Kissie's cocoa-colored shoulder.

"It's good to see you," Pastor Dev said as he came up for air. Then he turned to Lydia. "Lydia Cantrell, meet Kissie Pierre."

"Mercy me," Kissie said, grabbing Lydia by her

arm, her big dark eyes widening with glee, her gold bangles slipping down her arm. "You sure are a pretty little thing."

"Thank you," Lydia said, the heat of that praise causing her to blush. "And thank you for…helping us."

Kissie cluck-clucked that notion away. "Part of my job, honey-pie. That's why I'm here. Now y'all come on back to the kitchen and let me get some decent food and strong coffee in you."

Pastor Dev guided Lydia through the long, cluttered "club" part of the establishment. Lydia cast her gaze about, feeling as if she were in a forbidden zone. She saw reds and burgundies on the walls and in the furniture, plush Victorian sofas and dramatic Tiffany-style lamps, tassels and fringe in gold and bronze, and a huge white grand piano that sat in a prominent place by the floor-to-ceiling window in the front parlor. Across the squeaking, creaking worn wooden floor of the wide hallway, another room was filled with bistro tables and chairs and a gleaming mahogany bar along one wall. A huge sign running the length of the bar stated "Commit your work to the Lord, and your thoughts will be established." —Proverbs 16:3.

"I just don't get it," Lydia whispered, the paradox of this seemingly decadent place running amok in her pristine mind. "I don't see any alcohol behind that bar."

"That's the point," Pastor Dev said into her ear. "It's a cover, remember. The coffee bar works just fine. But Kissie makes it pretty clear that if you enter this establishment, it won't be to drink liquor and carry on. She offers tea, lemonade and a full range of coffees, as well as all kinds of sweet treats. It's more of a coffeehouse than a real bar, and her patrons know that."

"But Kissie has her faith right out there for all to see, right along with her dreadlocks and her coffee and chicory," Lydia retorted. "How can she get away with that and still run a blues club?"

"Kissie can be very persuasive. She's like a preacher and a party girl all rolled into one neat package. Since she also lets wayward teens live here, she won't allow any shenanigans. And that's what makes everyone love her so much," he said with a little grin. "Trust me."

There was that request again. Lydia thought about that, thought about Kissie and wondered how many strange people she was going to have to trust before this was all over. Her notion of a proper Christian included a church dress and a set of pearls—not a bright orange-and-brown silk caftan, shiny gold hoop earrings and two gold teeth to match.

But then, maybe her notions were just a bit narrow-minded and preconceived. Kissie did have a brilliant, loving smile and she had helped lots of people to the Lord, according to Pastor Dev.

Plus, her coffee smelled divine and those cinnamon rolls she slapped onto gold-edged china did look too good to pass up. When she added two slices of crisp bacon, Lydia decided Kissie was her new best friend.

"Thank you," Lydia said as Kissie handed her a cup of coffee and passed the cream. "I'm starving."

"'Course you are, child." Kissie glanced from Lydia to Pastor Dev, a serene smile on her face. Then she motioned for the teenage girl she'd called Jacqueline to leave the kitchen. Jacqueline gave them a blank look, but walked out of the room. Kissie waited a couple of seconds. "I've been briefed." Then she shrugged toward Lydia. "SOP."

"Standard operating procedure," Pastor Dev clarified.

"With a special urgency, of course," Kissie added, her voice low.

Lydia glanced up, amazed that the woman's laid-back tone had changed to all business now. Watching Pastor Dev and Kissie, she could tell things were about to get serious.

So she took a long drink of her coffee and let out a sigh of relief. For some strange reason, she did feel safe here in Kissie's Korner.

For now at least.

A couple of hours later, Dev peeked in on Lydia. She was sleeping in one of the dark-shaded upstairs bedrooms, her skin pale against the purple floral sheets and lavender satin comforter, her hair fanning out like golden-brown wheat against the shimmering pillow. Dev watched and listened, glad to hear her steady, peaceful breathing. Maybe she would get the rest she needed so much.

But there would be no rest for him.

So he headed downstairs to the room in the back that served as Kissie's office. The room with all the computers and monitors and cameras. The official CHAIM room.

"How's our baby girl?" Kissie asked as Dev entered the long, dark area that had once been a sleeping porch. Neither the sun nor the moon reached this place now. The area had been completely sealed off, a secret place hidden from most that frequented this establishment. There were no windows and a small door hidden behind a kitchen cabinet. Anyone who might notice would just think it was a storage room. Not even Lydia would see this dark corner.

"She's fast asleep."

Kissie nodded, causing her long braids to fall against her plump shoulder like fringe falling from an afghan. "Poor baby. This ain't easy."

"No," Dev said, closing his eyes to his own fatigue. "I'm sure the food and the hot shower helped."

"She'll be okay. I got a man posted nearby, watching. The whole system is on high alert, of course."

"Good. What's the word from upstairs?"

Kissie smiled at his reference. It was a little joke amongst the CHAIM team, and a gentle reminder that none of them was really in charge. God was their main boss.

"Well, the higher-ups are not happy. They believe one of their own has turned rogue. There's the law, and then there's the law of CHAIM, you understand?"

"Only too well," Dev replied, remembering his days as a full-time operative. One did not mess with the system. But apparently someone had.

"So do I have new orders?"

"To sit tight right now," Kissie replied over her shoulder as she hit buttons and flipped switches. "You'll receive word soon. But not here. The message will be posted at a different location. Probably somewhere else in the city." She sat down in front of a flickering computer monitor. "So, let's see the latest. We'll look for any unusual activity out there."

Dev watched as numbers and codes flashed by. "What if it's Eli, Kissie?"

"Of course it's Eli, honey," Kissie replied. "No one else would dare break the CHAIM brotherhood. But Eli always was a bit of a renegade, even after he turned his life over to the Lord. It makes sense that he'd be the one."

Dev ran a hand over his shower-damp hair. "Eli was one of us, one of the best. And because of me, he's out there on his own now. I can't decide if he's truly gone insane, or if he's just trying to get my attention."

"Murder could indicate both."

Dev stared at Kissie, the pain in her eyes matching what he felt in his heart. "I can't believe he'd deliberately murder someone—even me. It just doesn't add up. Whoever did this got the wrong man. That's not like Eli. He's more thorough. He wouldn't kill another person just to get to me. He'd just kill me and get it over with. But Eli was—is—a good man. Or at least he was until I blew the whistle on his extracurricular activities and ruined his life."

"It wasn't all your fault, Dev. Eli always had a dark streak a mile wide. We had to rein him in many a time, and you did the right thing by reporting him to our superiors. He was a walking time bomb."

"But look what it caused. I failed him. I wanted to get him some help, not turn him against all of us. I never dreamed it would lead to murder."

Kissie turned in her chair. "Are we talking about the current murder, Devon? Or the...other?"

"Both," Dev said, rubbing the back of his neck with his hand. "And they are both my fault."

"But you don't believe Eli actually committed *this* crime?"

Dev thought about that. "It's just a gut reaction. Eli is hurt and angry, and he's grieving. But he has the heart of a warrior—a Christian warrior. He wouldn't do something like this, but I believe his actions might have triggered it, somehow." He tapped his fingers on the sleek black desk. "And I believe something went wrong. Now Eli's on the run. He's either after me—and my hunch is wrong—or he wants to seek my help. Either way, he's going to be in big trouble when we find him." The tapping stopped. "And as we both know, CHAIM has its own system of justice."

Kissie's bright-red-painted nails hit the keys with precision. "I'll see what I can find out."

Dev watched as she typed in:

Pastoral, looking for a lost sheep. Please
respond ASAP.

"That's obvious," Dev said, shaking his head. "He
knows I'll be looking for him."

Then she wrote,

Judgment and justice take hold of you.

Dev understood the code. It was Kissie's way of
saying, "Don't take your own form of justice." And
they both knew that was exactly what Eli specialized
in. Even after rigorous training, Eli still had a vigilante streak.

Then she wrote,

Do not walk with wicked men.

Dev knew that Job was CHAIM's special book of
the Bible, the one the organization used to talk in
code. Would Eli, known as The Disciple, see the
codes embedded in their main Web site and know
Dev was trying to reach out to him? Or would this
bring Eli right to Kissie's door? Eli was smart enough
to break through the encryptions and find the exact
location of the router. He would be here within hours
if that happened. Maybe that needed to happen, and
if Lydia wasn't here with him, Dev would almost
welcome that confrontation. Once and for all.

Dev thought about the woman sleeping upstairs
and vowed he couldn't let that happen just yet. Not

until Lydia was safe. "What now?" he asked after Kissie keyed in a few more carefully worded messages.

"We wait," she said, her dark eyes giving him a sharp look. "And you try to get some sleep." When he looked doubtful, she added, "Don't worry. I rerouted everything and it's all encrypted. It will only reach those who might be looking for it, and those who know where to look. I believe Eli is good at that sort of thing, but if he's smart, he won't come near New Orleans right now." Then she got up, pushing him toward the door. "Rest."

"I can't sleep," Dev replied. "I have to watch."

"And pray," Kissie added with a soft smile.

"Who's on the agenda for tonight?" he asked, hoping for a diversion.

"The Gospel According to Pauly."

He nodded, flexed the tight muscles in his back. "I love that band. Perfect harmony of all the oldies but goodies."

"Good, solid gospel and soul," Kissie said, getting up to shuffle some printouts. "Can't go wrong with that mix."

"I need a good mix to get us out of this mess," Dev said as they exited the room. "Of course, Lydia and I might have to miss the show."

"We'll see, once we receive your next orders."

After they'd safely secured the secret entranceway, Kissie turned to face him. "Pastoral, you did everything in your power to keep Eli on the straight and narrow. The Disciple has strayed on his own. He didn't seek help. In fact, he refused any help…after the South America incident."

"But he went through his own form of grief and repentance," Dev said, his voice low. "He went into seclusion, but it was at CHAIM's demand. It was the best thing he could do, but Eli would have chafed under that sentence. And he would have plotted."

"Well, now he's out," Kissie said with a pragmatic shrug. "And apparently, his time to reflect *didn't* help him. He's not well, Devon."

Dev's palm hit the granite counter. "That's because the man is heartbroken, Kissie. We destroyed—"

"Destroyed what?"

Dev turned to see Lydia standing at the arched doorway to the kitchen, her hair cascading around her pale face. "What did you destroy, Pastor Dev? Or is that information classified?"

Everything around here was classified, Lydia decided later. Pastor Dev had refused to clue her in, for her own protection, of course. So she'd spent most of the afternoon either napping underneath one of the many ceiling fans around the big house, or reading one of the many interesting books and magazines Kissie kept stashed in her upstairs living quarters. The woman had everything from *O* magazine to the *Wall Street Journal* and *People* magazine, not to mention various forms of Christian fiction and nonfiction.

Lydia had read an entire *O* from cover to cover—

some of those life lessons in there were pretty good. Then she'd skimmed all the celebrity rags—her daddy wouldn't approve of that—and read a short inspirational romance that had a nice, sweet, happily-ever-after ending.

And wondered if she'd ever have the same.

Then she'd visited with the two girls living here under Kissie's supervision. Jacqueline was moody and resentful. She hated the foster home system. Amy was sweet and unassuming. She loved being safe here with Kissie. Both had been caught up in bad situations. Jacqueline, alcohol and boys; Amy, in an abusive, drug-infested home. They'd been careful not to reveal too much to Lydia, but they'd plied her with curious questions about everything from her favorite songs to what type of perfume and makeup she liked. Careful to be honest but not too forthcoming, Lydia had indulged in a little girl talk until Jacqueline had gone upstairs to clean and Amy had left to run an errand.

Afterward, bored and looking for something to distract her from all her worries, Lydia had explored the old house, and found all sorts of nooks and crannies. This place was one part history, one part cabaret and one part haven.

"Lord, I hope you have a sense of humor," Lydia said to herself now as she slowly made her way down the long staircase. Determined to question Pastor Dev again, she decided to look for him. Both he and Kissie could get gone faster than humanly possible, but Lydia reckoned that was a CHAIM trait. She also knew that even though the two were as thick as thieves and up to their elbows in espionage, they had others stationed here and there, watching out for Lydia. Or as she'd heard Pastor Dev whispering to Kissie, "Keeping visuals." She had to be in someone's line of sight at all times, apparently.

That would explain the tiny cameras hidden everywhere. She'd found them in lamps and in pictures, in plants and in the intricate crown molding on some of the walls.

Not only was this whole house equipped with more cameras than the Pentagon, but Kissie also employed a lot of hardworking, very observant people.

A petite little maid here, dusting and watching.

A nice elderly gardener there, clipping hedges and waiting.

A cable repairman on the roof, realigning the satellite dish while he did a little recon work on the entire neighborhood.

"I didn't just fall off the turnip truck," Lydia said out loud, then instantly wished she hadn't when she spotted Pastor Dev at the bottom of the stairs, smiling up at her.

"Well, if you did, that must have been one pretty turnip crop."

Lydia tried not to blush. "You shouldn't sneak up on a girl that way."

The smile faded away. "Sorry, old habits die hard."

That was sure the truth. Come to think of it, Lydia

and the church staff had all been amazed at how quietly this man could enter a room. Now she understood why, at least.

She met him at the bottom of the stairs, then plopped down. "I don't like being idle. Idleness is the devil's workshop."

He tilted his head and gave her a sideways glance. "The devil would have his hands full with you, Lydia."

"I'd give him a run for his money, that's for sure."

She liked the way he smiled at her. His smile made him look so young and carefree, the way he used to look before all of this, back when she thought he was just a kindly minister. "You seem in a better mood."

He sat down beside her, then stretched his jean-clad legs out over the stairs. "This place makes me feel safe."

"Me, too," she admitted. "How long have you known Kissie?"

"Since I attended seminary here in New Orleans. She was one of our special instructors."

"Get out? What did she teach you—the history of blues?"

He laughed at that. "Kissie is a computer whiz. That's her specialty. But you wouldn't know it to look at her."

Lydia grinned at that. "Not your average professor type."

"No, not at all. She was one of the first people I met when I was…introduced into CHAIM."

Lydia was dying to hear the whole, long, drawn-out story, but she didn't want to break the gentle truce of this quiet summer afternoon. Sitting here, she could almost believe they were just visiting New Orleans on vacation. But she did ask one burning question. "What if you'd said no to CHAIM? Would they have burned you at the stake or something?"

"You have a vivid imagination."

"Just curious."

"No, nothing so bad. They would have let me get on with my life. And it would been as if—"

"As if you'd never heard of them, right?"

He touched his arm to hers, poking at her, a grin on his face. "You're learning."

Lydia felt the burn of that playful touch all the way to her toes. It made her edgy and antsy, so she got up. "I need something to do. And don't tell me there isn't anything to do. I see all these people pretending to work around here, that is, while they keep watching me. It's getting on my last nerve."

As if on cue, Kissie came bustling around the corner. "I got something for you to do, child."

"Great," Lydia said, pushing her hair back behind her ears. "I can sort mail, make some calls, file some papers—"

"No, no, honey," Kissie said with a grin. "This is a special project. We're gonna give you a good and proper makeover."

Lydia glanced from Kissie's expectant face to Pastor Dev's blank one. "I don't want a makeover."

"You need a cover," Kissie explained. "They know what you look like now, honey."

"How do you know that?"

Pastor Dev got up, let out a sigh as if to say, Break time is over now. "We've received reports. CHAIM now has a dossier on you. And that means so do the bad guys, probably. We can't take any chances."

Lydia slapped a hand against the newel post. "Well, that's just lovely. How exciting for CHAIM— and the bad guys." She'd have to record all of this in her diary immediately so she'd have her own report. "So, what now?"

"Now," Kissie said, a firm hand on Lydia's arm, "we change your looks. Amy just got back with our ammunition."

Lydia held to the post. "I don't want to change my looks. I like me the way I am, thank you. And I don't need any ammunition."

Dev took her other arm. "Lydia, do this, please. For me. We have to blend in and look the part."

"What part?"

"That of a very wealthy, happily married couple."

Lydia's knees seemed to turn to mush. Holding tightly to the newel post, she glanced from Kissie to Pastor Dev. "You and me, you mean?"

"You and me," he said, a soft smile creaking across his face. "I need you to cooperate, please."

She could see the no-arguing look in his eyes, and she could certainly hear the commando mode in his words, but how could she resist the opportunity to pretend to be his wife, just for one night? Hiding her secret glee behind a show of agitation, she said, "I guess I don't have much of a choice, do I? Just like

I didn't have a choice in coming here, or a choice in being in that room at the wrong time, right?"

"I'm sorry," he said, the apology darkening his eyes. "We have to protect you."

That caused her glee to dissipate. "But I thought I was safe here."

"You are, for now," Pastor Dev explained. "But we can't stay here forever. And later tonight we have to go out and do some…research. That's why we need to dress you up, so to speak."

"So it's like I'm playing a spy part or something?"

"Something," Pastor Dev said, nodding. "At first, I thought I'd just leave you in a safe place. But I've reconsidered that. I don't want you out of my sight. You have to be by my side at all times so I can protect you. Tonight, we have to look like a couple."

"Is that an order?"

"It's a request."

Lydia didn't know whether to laugh or cry. She'd always dreamed of being by his side at all times. But never like this. His *request* sure put her in a pickle. "I see," she said, not really seeing at all. "So who do I get to be? Lois Lane, Catwoman, Mary Poppins, maybe?"

Kissie let out a hoot of laughter. "She's a live wire, this one. Pastoral, you may have just met your match."

Lydia looked over at Pastor Dev, their eyes meeting in the brilliance of the golden dusk that filtered its way throughout the house. The look he gave her sent shards of hope and longing through Lydia's heart. He looked sweet and unsure. But Lydia was very sure she was the woman who would love him and stay by his side at all times, for the rest of their lives, however long that might turn out to be.

"Let's get this over with," she said to break the spell of his powerful gaze. "I don't have all day, after all."

Kissie laughed again, then shook her head. "You gonna be just fine, honey-pie. Just fine. We'll get you all fixed up and pretty for this high-society party tonight."

Lydia shot Pastor Dev a questioning look. He didn't seem as confident as Kissie. He looked downright worried. But Lydia couldn't be sure if it was because someone was trying to do him in, or because he'd just realized Kissie might be right. Maybe he had finally met his match.

SIX

Dev waited, pacing at the bottom of the stairs, for Lydia and Kissie to come down. It was almost dark now; the New Orleans dusk was alive with the sounds and scents of nature. Jasmine and magnolias competed with honeysuckle and hibiscus, their sweet, cloying fragrances merging into a sultry perfume. Blue jays and sparrows made swishing sounds in the big live oak by the back gate, while squirrels chased each other in the banana fronds near the water garden in the courtyard. And somewhere, a mockingbird lifted its voice to the sky.

He wished he could let these things distract him. But his mind was on this mission and the woman he had to protect. And from the sounds of feminine giggles and gasps upstairs, that woman had just undergone an amazing transformation.

Which was why he was now pacing and sweating in the hall, while the gospel group set up in the big coffee bar.

Devon Malone had scaled ten-foot walls to save

human lives; he'd walked through fire to rescue trapped missionaries from rebels and drug lords. He'd swum through alligator-infested swamps to get to another person in need. He'd been shot at, attacked, taken hostage, stabbed, robbed, beaten and left for dead.

But none of that had ever prepared him for Lydia Cantrell.

Her very innocence and sweetness took his breath away.

And now, because of him, she was about to change. She would not be so innocent from now on. Who knew what this journey would do to her delicate, sweet nature. Or to his own frazzled, confused mind. He'd always considered Lydia a dear friend and a wonderful office assistant. He'd taken her for granted for so long now, he automatically kept her front and center in his thoughts all day long.

Only now, she was invading his nighttime thoughts, too. That was certainly understandable, under the circumstances. He had to protect her. He'd done this kind of operation a hundred times over. He'd been assigned to escort important people before, had played bodyguard to ministers' wives and children all over the world. But he'd never actually cared too deeply about those people, other than an abiding Christian love for his fellow man, and because of the pledge he'd made to protect human life when he'd joined CHAIM.

But Lydia was…well, she was Lydia. Solid and sure, pragmatic and practical, cute and lovely, pretty and so very sweet. Lydia was the girl next door, the good and proper young lady, the person he considered not only a friend but a valuable member of his church and his staff.

So when had he starting noticing things like her pretty, pouting lips and her soft, shimmering blond-brown hair? And those big hazel eyes, always changing colors like a kaleidoscope, so bright and trusting, so confused and questioning. When had he started wanting to get to know her on a more intimate level—all things Lydia, all things about her life and her hopes? How had he not seen the radiance of her smile before? And why did that smile tug at his heart so much now?

It's because you have to protect her, he told himself as he paced over the soft, faded fleur-de-lis patterned wool rug that covered the downstairs entryway, the sound of a saxophone warming up drifting around him. After all, close proximity always brought out feelings of protection, didn't it? Being with another person so many hours of the day caused one to discover the most interesting things about that person.

Such as that cute little mole on her right cheek. And her endearing dimples. And the way she lifted her dark eyebrows each time she doubted him.

Which seemed to be a lot lately.

Devon had to rein in all the emotions rushing through his system. Of course, he cared about Lydia. She was one of his flock. She was a dear friend. She was—

"Beautiful." The word came out of his mouth as he glanced up to find Lydia standing at the top of the stairs, a hesitant, scared look on her face.

Her very different face.

Her hair was now highlighted with soft hues of blond. Kissie had trimmed it into a long shag of some sort. Little wisps fell around Lydia's face and across her brow. Her eyebrows, lifting now in another kind of doubt, had been shaped and trimmed to make them even more alluring and intriguing. She wore makeup, something Lydia rarely did. But it wasn't too fussy or heavy. Just a little shimmer of glitter here, a bit of gloss there. The smoky hues around her vivid eyes made them look the color of rich bronze. Her whole look had changed to the point that not even he could have recognized her out on the street. That would serve their purposes, but Dev almost regretted this change.

Except for the dress. Though modestly cut, the dress was over the top, even for Kissie. And it looked great on Lydia.

"I can't leave the house wearing this," Lydia said as she traipsed down the stairs on her new high-heeled sandals. "If my daddy saw me—"

"Your daddy's not here," Dev said in a husky voice, wishing he hadn't even thought that. He had to turn around, take a breath. Pushing a hand through his hair, he struggled for control. Then he felt a hand on his shoulder. He whirled, ready to do battle. Then he let out a sigh. Kissie had managed to sneak up on him.

"You're losing it," she whispered. "Get yourself together."

He nodded, turned to face Lydia, who was now on the bottom step of the stairs. She was getting as good at this stealth business as the rest of them.

"I look awful, don't I?" she said, tears welling in her eyes. "I'm not…this is not me…I don't know if I can—"

Dev glanced over at Kissie and saw the warning look in her eyes. He needed to say exactly the right thing. "Lydia," he began, his words sounding shaky but growing firm with each syllable, "you look… amazing. The dress is very attractive and necessary. Now be a good girl, and just go with it."

Lydia came down the last step to glare at him, so close now he could smell the scent of lily of the valley. Kissie sure did like floral perfumes. "Go with it? I look like a floozy and you know it."

"No, you don't," he said, meaning it. "You could never look that way. You look like you, only different. I like the hair. You look like a proper society lady."

"But this dress…" She looked down at the shimmering, slinking fabric that fell straight and fitted to just below her knees. "I tried another one, but it was way too short. At least this one is a decent length. But this red, beaded stuff…it's just not me."

Dev whirled on Kissie. "Is that the only dress you could find?"

"In her size, yes, sir," Kissie replied, all business. "It's this or nothing. And we have to remember, she has to be dressed to the nines to fit the part. And so do you, so you're next. Upstairs, now."

Dev focused on the assignment, tearing his eyes away from Lydia. "What…what am I wearing tonight?" he managed to ask, gazing at Lydia's pretty eyes, accentuated by her hair.

"A tux," Kissie said. "Y'all are set to attend a masquerade party in the Garden District. Some big shot is throwing it for a group of important out-of-town visitors, if you get my drift. Your presence has been requested."

Dev understood. He would meet one of his superiors at this party and receive further instructions. CHAIM had operatives in all sorts of places—governments, churches, businesses, university systems, hospitals—you name it. It gave new meaning to the term "never alone."

"I'll just go get ready," he said, giving Lydia one last glance. Then he touched a hand to her arm. "Lydia, you look beautiful. I promise."

Lydia didn't look convinced. "Is it too…risqué?"

"Not on you," he replied, smiling for the first time since she'd come down the stairs. "It just looks… good."

"And you get to carry a feathered mask, too," Kissie added. "I'll give that to you when you get ready to leave."

She finally let out a sigh of relief. "I guess I can pull this off. I'm just not used to fancy threads and too much makeup."

"It becomes you," Dev said again, to reassure her.

"If you feel uncomfortable, just keep your mask over your face."

"Hiding behind a mask—that just about sums this up," Lydia said, resolve coloring her expression. "Go on and get ready. I'll be okay."

Her tentative smile captivated him, so he tried again to reassure her. "I'll make sure of that, I promise."

But as he hurried up the stairs, he knew this wasn't about reassurance. Lydia Cantrell might have been plain and simple before all of this, and that had been just fine with him. But now, she was a knockout, a beautiful, attractive woman.

And that wasn't just fine with him. Because it was causing him to be careless. And CHAIM didn't allow for carelessness. He had to stay focused on the mission, on protecting Lydia.

And that meant he couldn't think about things that were inappropriate and risky, such as kissing her, or holding her close, or taking her out for a real romantic dinner. So he turned at the top of the stairs and looked down on her as she stood in the middle of the hallway, taking once last glimpse at her—just to get her out of his mind.

In the coffee bar, the gospel singers started a rendition of "Softly and Tenderly." The old hymn was all about Jesus calling all sinners to come home. But for Dev, the terms softly and tenderly also described how he felt about Lydia. He never wanted to see her hurt, or worse, dead. Which was why he had to remain distant and professional. Until he could have her safely home.

Her gaze caught his, held him there, held him captive with sweetness and temptation. He gripped the old oak banister in order to control his emotions. And his longings. Then, reminding himself he had a job to do, he hurried away and slammed the door to his room.

Lydia turned to Kissie, her heart pounding with uncertainty. "This is so embarrassing. He doesn't approve. He's not used to seeing me like this."

"You can sure say that again," Kissie replied, a wry twinkle in her eyes.

Amy came downstairs, her smile sweet and shy. "I'm done straightening Lydia's room now, Miss Kissie."

"Thanks, honey. Go on in the kitchen and get you some supper."

Amy, all pale and blond and wearing baggy khakis and a worn T-shirt, glanced over at Lydia. "You look great."

"Thank you," Lydia said, "and thanks for all your help." Amy had helped with her makeup and had even suggested she put on some perfume. Deciding earlier to use lotion instead of the heavy spray concentrate, Lydia now hoped the lily scent didn't provoke her allergies.

Amy nodded, then strolled toward the back of the house. But she turned at the door to the kitchen, her blue eyes going wide. "Take care, Lydia."

Kissie added an "Amen" to that.

"I need to change," Lydia said, moving toward the

stairs. The high-heeled, glittery sandals were not so easy to move around in. "I can't do this. I just can't."

"Child, stop right there," Kissie said, grabbing her by the arm with a mighty firm hold. "You gonna be fine. That man more than approves of the way you look. He's just having to get used to the new you, on top of all his other problems. And we don't need you adding to that load."

"I'm not planning on staying this way," Lydia declared, determination making her voice rise. "And I'm trying very hard *not* to *be* a problem. Why can't I just stay here, safe and sound? I'd stay out of the way. I could read a good book and go to bed early. I'll write in my journal and read my Bible. I'm behind on my devotionals anyway."

Kissie shook her head. "Can't let you. Devon wants you with him at all times. He knows it's his responsibility to protect you."

"But why do I have to be someone I'm not?"

"Part of the game, honey. Our contact can't just show up here at my door, so we have to send you to this party, partly to throw them off, and partly to keep our operatives secret. An exchange will be made, information given over. If they're watching, which we're pretty sure they are, they won't recognize Devon and you—or they won't expect you to show up at this party. The element of surprise and all that. It's important to blend in with the crowd and look as if you belong, and they won't expect a sweet thing like you to look like that, trust me."

"I don't plan on staying like this, and I mean it,"

Lydia repeated, crossing her arms in a stubborn stance.

"Nobody said you have to stay this way," Kissie replied in a calm, serene voice. "In fact, this is probably just the first of many disguises. But the haircut is cute. And the makeup does play up your pretty eyes. And the dress…well, that's just for show and just for tonight. You do not look like a floozy, okay? Kissie don't do floozy, all right?"

"I didn't mean to insult you," Lydia said, embarrassment causing her skin to heat up. "I've just never worn anything so fancy and so…clingy."

"I'm not offended," Kissie said. "I'm having a good time. Haven't seen this many fireworks since Christmas down on the river."

"Fireworks?" Lydia looked around, confused as usual.

"Girl, you don't see it, do you?" Kissie chuckled then started toward the coffee bar. "I got to get ready for the gospel crowd. They're already pouring in." She waved a hand toward the coffee bar. "We should have a full house tonight."

Lydia followed her, just to keep busy. "I'll help."

"Not in that, you won't."

"What did you mean, that I don't see it?"

Kissie turned at the long counter. "That man up there. He…he's got a clear thing for you, honey."

Lydia's heart bounced and lifted like a string of beads being tossed through the air, then righted itself. "He…we're…coworkers and fellow Christians, so yes, I'm sure he cares about me through the love of Christ."

Kissie grinned. "Yeah, right. Baby, there is the love of Christ, and then there is the love of a man for a woman. Maybe you're both blind to it."

Lydia knew how *she* felt, but it had never occurred to her that Pastor Dev might have even the tiniest bit of an inkling of returning those feelings. "Are you saying—"

Kissie held up a jewel bedecked hand. "I'm just saying something's brewing in this place besides the coffee, understand?"

Lydia smiled then, gaining a new confidence. "I think I just might."

Kissie gave her a long, intense look. "Good, then. 'Cause the better you understand Devon Malone, the more able you'll be when the time comes for him to reach out to you. He's gonna need someone strong when this is all over. You just might be the one."

Lydia let the echo of that prediction reverberate throughout her system. Then she remembered last night and how he'd cried in her arms. How he'd looked into her eyes as if he were a drowning man. A woman didn't forget a look like that. A woman didn't forget a man like Pastor Dev.

"I'll be here, always," she told Kissie. "You have my word on that."

"I never doubted it," Kissie said with a soft smile.

Lydia took a seat on one of the plush settees and waited for Pastor Dev, her thoughts going from a working relationship to something more meaningful and deep. Closing her eyes, she let the soothing praise music coming from the next room help to calm her frazzled nerves.

Could it be so, Lord? she asked, prayed, hoped. Did the man she love also love her back? Well, he was going through a whole heap of trouble to protect her. And he did have about a million burdens on his mind. Maybe it was simply being thrown together. That alone was enough to make him more protective and considerate.

Lydia thought about that angle, and decided instead of whining and fighting him at every turn, she would try really hard to be more cooperative. She wouldn't be any trouble at all. She'd do everything he said so that they could get back home to Dixon and the work of the church.

And then, once all of this was behind them and they were back on a routine, she'd see if Pastor Devon Malone still looked at her the way he'd looked at her tonight. And she'd find out if it mattered whether she was wearing a red dress or not.

SEVEN

Lydia realized two things as she looked through the eye slits of her red-sequined feathered mask at the formal parlor of the elegant Garden District antebellum mansion. One, she was way out of her league with all these rich folks wearing real diamonds and fake smiles. And two, Pastor Dev sure looked good in a tuxedo and a black satin mask.

The big white-columned two-storied house had to be well over one hundred years old. The furnishings were all priceless antiques. And Lydia knew antiques from living over her Aunt Mabel's Antique Depot. The names Hepplewhite, Chippendale, Windsor and Duncan Phyfe floated through her mind as she admired the huge sideboards and buffets loaded with food and the gleaming secretary sitting in one corner, a crystal bowl of floating magnolia blossoms its only adornment. She was pretty sure the ornate burgundy-and-gold strung rug in the parlor was an aged Aubusson. And the artwork and knickknacks indicated an eclectic taste, with a mixture of old world style and modern abstracts vying for the attention of the dressy crowd.

The French doors on every side of the long square house were thrown open to the mild summer night, while ancient ceiling fans hummed and swirled, bringing down refreshing breezes from the high, ornately scrolled ceilings. Classical music wafted out over the wind, courtesy of a string quartet centered on one of the long verandas.

Lydia tried to concentrate on her surroundings and not on the man who'd gone to find them some fresh lemonade. But Pastor Dev was back, right at her side. In fact, he'd somehow managed to keep his gaze on her as he'd crossed the dining room to the huge punch bowl centered on the long Queen Anne table. She'd watched him, their eyes meeting in spite of the masks they both wore.

"Here you go," he said, handing her a dainty crystal cup of the chilled lemonade concoction. Then he reached his other hand around. "I found some brownies, too. I know you love brownies."

Lydia could have kissed the man, but then that probably wasn't such a good idea, considering all the erratic thoughts moving with the same whirl as the ceiling fans through her mind. "Thank you." She took a bite of a moist chocolate square, and closed her eyes. "You know, I have to say that the eating on this particular little adventure has been fine so far. I'm not starving."

"No, you're not," he said, his eyes sweeping over her face for reassurance. "You look fit as a fiddle."

Lydia laughed at that, and then flushed. "Nothing wrong with my appetite."

"Sorry." He gulped his own lemonade, as he looked around. "I would have thought we'd make contact by now."

Lydia smiled at the way he looked all flustered and embarrassed, and the way he had quickly changed from flirtatious to commando in order to hide his own discomfort. That was rather endearing. But then she remembered the circumstances. Best not to flirt. Best to concentrate on staying alive.

"This mask is making my face itch," she said after she'd swallowed the last of her brownie. "Can't we find a corner so we can take these things off for a minute or two?"

"Not until after our contact approaches us."

"Any idea who we're looking for?"

"No. That's how things go with CHAIM. It's so secretive and undercover, that I might not even see the operative. But I'll get the message. A word here, a gesture there."

"Well, that should be easy."

He laughed at her smirk. "No, the easy part is spending time with you. You look right at home here, Lydia."

She rolled her eyes, even though she wasn't sure if he noticed. "Yeah, right. I am not to the manor born, Pastor Dev, as you well know."

He shook his head. "You could be, though."

"Thank you," Lydia said, deciding to just accept his compliment. She finished off another brownie.

"Wow, I must have eaten that too fast. I feel a little funny." She touched a finger to the scratchy stitching and feathers at her temple. "My face feels so warm."

Pastor Dev immediately became concerned. "Maybe it's the heat."

"I'm not hot," she replied. She felt chills sweeping through her body even as she said the words. She'd felt chilled earlier, but just figured it was because of the cross ventilation from the open doors and the competent ceiling fans. "Maybe I just need to sit down."

He took her cup and set it on a nearby tray. "Let's go out on the veranda."

Lydia nodded. She didn't want to alarm him, but her skin did feel all clammy and hot now. She went from chills to what felt like fever, back and forth. She wondered if she'd eaten too much sugar. She did have a big sweet tooth.

"Sit here," he told her as he urged her down onto a lacy white bistro chair in one corner of the planked porch, away from the crowd at the big double entry doors. "There's a nice breeze here by this big magnolia tree."

"Thank you." Lydia sat down, careful to pull her dress around her knees. She breathed in the fragrant lemony scent of the magnolias, then swallowed back the nausea in her stomach. "I'll be fine. Just got a bit too stuffy in there."

"Here, get this thing off your face," he said, tugging at her disguise. Slipping it over her head, he stared straight into her eyes. "You don't look so good."

Lydia waved a hand, trying to make a joke. "Not what I expected when I revealed my identity to you at last, kind sir."

Pastor Dev shook his head, smiling slightly, then he looked around, a frown replacing his smile. "I'm going to try and make contact so we can get out of here and get you home to rest." Then he put his hands on his hips as he gave her a once-over. "But I don't want to leave you."

"I'm fine, really," Lydia said. "It's nice out here, and now that I've removed all those feathers away from my face, I don't feel so scratchy."

"I still can't leave you alone." He stood over her, protective and hovering. Then in frustration, he yanked off his own simple black mask. In spite of the situation, that made her smile. Then she glanced across the porch and saw a tall, distinguished-looking man staring at her through an elaborate swirling silver domino. Lydia smiled at him. He smiled back. Then he started toward them. Maybe Pastor Dev wouldn't have to leave her.

"Pastor Dev," Lydia said under her breath, "we might have company."

Dev glanced around, his actions carefully controlled. "Okay. Let's see what happens." Then he leaned close and slipped his mask back on, then handed Lydia hers. "We have to pretend we don't see him. Don't be obvious." After she grudgingly put her domino back on, he whispered into her ear. "Look at me."

Lydia did as he asked, glad to have the excuse. "Did I tell you that you look nice in that tux?"

"No, you didn't. But thanks." He touched a finger to a stray wisp of hair near her temple. "Is he still coming toward us?"

Lydia made a quick scan of the verandah, her shivers now coming from Pastor Dev's touch. She quickly reminded herself that this was just playacting. The man moved right past them, and didn't even bother looking back. But Lydia felt the brush of air as he casually walked by, then strolled down the steps into the big front yard.

"He was right there, but I don't see him anymore." Then she looked back up at Pastor Dev, blinking because she was suddenly seeing two of him.

Dev turned again, discreetly showing her a folded note. "He left us his calling card right here in the potted plant."

Lydia giggled. "You people actually do that— leave things in the potted plants?"

"I know—it's so cliché, but it worked. Neither of us even saw him do it, but I certainly saw the note lying there when I turned."

"Glad you're the one who found it." She swallowed the ache in her throat and croaked, "What does it say?"

He read it to her in a soft whisper. "'The eagle dwells on the rock. Go to the eagle.'"

"I guess that's from Job, too, more or less? What does that mean?"

He leaned close, so the casual observer would

think he was filling her ear with sweet talk. "It means we're going to be traveling again. I know where we need to go now, to keep you safe."

"How—" Lydia tried to form the words, but her heart rate accelerated too fast, causing her to feel faint. "Oh, boy," she said, grabbing for his arm.

"Lydia?"

She heard Pastor Dev's voice, but she couldn't seem to focus on his words. She tried to stand. "I don't feel so good."

He caught her to him. "Lydia, are you sick?"

She tried to nod. Her skin felt as if it were on fire. "Hot." Then she pushed at him as shivers moved up and down her arms. "Cold."

Pastor Dev grabbed her by the waist. "Lean on me."

She tried to do that, but everything was becoming murky. She couldn't focus. "Hot…cold." The chills and fever seemed to be warring with her skin, raking her with heat followed by ice. The fire of it hissed over her arms, her neck, her face. "Must be having an allergic reaction."

Another man came to them. Lydia vaguely recognized him as the Distinguished Gentleman who'd just brushed past with the note. Their contact? Or the enemy? Had he been watching after he left the note?

"Come with me," he said over her head to Dev.

"I don't think—"

"You'd better listen," the man told Dev. "Come with me now. I just got a message from the Lady at the Well. She was afraid to call your line."

Dev nodded. "Lydia, can you walk?"

"I think so." She wanted to sit back down and rub this fire off her skin. "Hot. Fire."

Dev spoke into her ear. "Just hang on, honey. You're having some sort of reaction. We'll take care of you, but we have to be very discreet."

Lydia knew the drill. He didn't want to bring any more attention to them. Even in her frenzied state of mind, she could sense his anxiety. So she managed a smile. "Let me go," she whispered to both of the men. "I can get through that side door over there around the corner. No one will notice."

Dev shot a glance toward the back of the wrap-around veranda, where a French door stood open. "She's right. No one is looking at us and no one is roaming back there. If we take her through the front, everyone will notice."

The gray-haired man nodded, his eyes calm and sure through the slits of his mask. "I agree. Okay, let's smile and laugh, just in case."

Lydia did laugh. She laughed because her skin felt as if a million fire ants were crawling over her. She laughed because she knew she was in serious trouble and that something had gone terribly wrong some-where between the limo ride and the lemonade. She even laughed at the note in the potted plant. Another good one for her journal.

Then she stopped laughing, the heat of the big, bright blue bedroom they'd stumbled into causing her to want to throw up. "Did I do something wrong?" she asked Pastor Dev, her eyes brimming with frustrated tears. "I did something wrong." She tugged her mask off and threw it on the floor.

He sat her down in a blue brocade wing chair, his hand touching on the pulse at her wrist. "No, sweetheart, you did everything just right."

She gulped back a sob. "You called me sweetheart."

He tossed his mask down next to hers. "Yes, I sure did."

She lifted her gaze to his face, but he was staring over at the other man. "Her pulse is erratic. What did Kissie report?"

Distinguished Gentleman shook his head, which made him look like a gargoyle with that creepy mask shimmering in gray and silver. "It seems we've been compromised. She wouldn't tell me. You need to call her."

"I'll secure the line." Pastor Dev got out his trusty phone, punching codes while his gaze and one hand stayed on Lydia. "Hold on, honey."

He was being awfully sweet, Lydia thought, her hands scraping at her burning skin. "I need...I'm hot, so hot." She tried to speak, but her throat seemed to be closing up.

"Kissie?"

Pastor Dev listened, then hissed a breath. "I'm on it." He hung up, stared across at the other man. "I need a bathroom."

Lydia started giggling. "Me, too, come to think of it. Too much lemonade."

"It's not the lemonade," Dev said. "It's the

perfume. She's wearing lily of the valley." He was speaking to Distinguished Gentleman, Lydia noted, but she heard him loud and clear. "Amy poisoned the perfume—Kissie thinks it was pesticide. We have to get her washed down."

Lydia's head came up. "Me? You have to wash *me* down?"

Pastor Dev helped her up as the other man motioned toward a bathroom just off the bedroom, then headed off in that direction. "Yes, Lydia. You've absorbed some sort of bug spray through your perfume—pesticides. That's what's making you sick."

She registered that, then added, "Amy? But Amy was the nice one. She was so sweet."

"Not that sweet," Pastor Dev said through gritted teeth. "She's high now. She traded information for drugs, apparently. Then she agreed to poison you, probably for even more drugs. But Kissie managed to get the truth out of her."

"Oh, no. The VEPs got to Amy. Poor Amy."

Distinguished Gentleman looked confused, "Who—"

"Very Evil People," she said to him over her shoulder as Pastor Dev gathered her up. He lifted her into his arms, then headed toward the bathroom, but Lydia couldn't enjoy his touch—it hurt her skin to be touched. Then she heard water being turned on, but that didn't bother her half as much as the white-hot pokers branding her skin and the fact that Pastor Dev had her in his arms and drat, she couldn't even enjoy it.

"Ugh, pesticides?" she said, her fingers scratching at her burning, itching skin. "I'm allergic to things like that. Hives. I told Amy—I told Amy I couldn't wear strong perfume. I used the lotion, because the perfume made me sneeze. I only used the lotion. I get the hives if it's too strong."

"This will be more than hives if we don't hurry," Distinguished Gentleman said. "Most common pesticides don't cause an immediate reaction, but we don't know how much she's been exposed or how long, especially if the girl put it in the lotion. And we don't have much time before they find out where you two are. This might help temporarily, but she will still need medical help."

"Do we have people posted?" Dev asked.

"Yes. I'll alert them immediately." Then the man nodded toward Lydia. "You take care of her."

Pastor Dev put one hand on her chin. "I'm sorry to have to do this, Lydia. Please forgive me."

And then Lydia felt the warm wash of water hitting her in the face, along with Pastor Dev's hands on her shoulders, holding her under the shower spray.

"Let me go," she cried out, the lukewarm water merging with the agony racing down her body. Her skin was raw with pain and heat, tears were streaming down her face, and she wanted to be somewhere else. Somewhere safe. So she tried to pound that thought into him as she hit against his chest. "Let me go."

But he didn't let her go.

Instead, he got inside the open shower with her, both of them fully clothed, and held her so tightly that soon they were both completely soaked, too.

Lydia looked at him, sobs moving throughout her body, the sensation of being burned alive clawing at her flesh. "What's wrong with me? What did they do to me?"

He held her face in his hands, his eyes focused on hers. "Listen to me. You're going to be all right, Lydia. I promise. I promise."

"You always promise so much," she said, angry now. Angry with him, and with CHAIM, and with the world in general. "You always promise, but...I'm hurting. I'm hurting." She realized she was screaming now, but she didn't care. "So don't make me any more promises, all right?"

"All right," he said, his voice low and calm, even though his eyes blazed with the same tears and frustrations she felt. And the same rage. "All right. No more promises."

And then he kissed her.

EIGHT

He'd had no other choice, Dev kept telling himself as he kissed Lydia, and he kept right on kissing her long after she'd stopped pounding her tiny fists into his chest. Long after she'd slumped against him and settled into his embrace. He probably would have continued, since her lips had gone warm and tender, if they hadn't been interrupted by their gray-haired friend.

"You must leave. Now!"

That urgent command brought Dev back to full alert. And made him realize that once again, he'd been distracted enough to put Lydia in even more danger. But she had been near hysterics, so what else could he have done? He wouldn't strike a woman. Kissing her quiet had seemed the best plan at the time. But now…

Their helper turned off the water and tossed a big towel at Lydia. "Get her out of there."

"What's going on?" Lydia asked, her eyes dazed, her skin flushed. Chill bumps dotted her arms.

Dev pulled her out onto the tiled floor and tugged the big pink towel around her ruined dress. "C'mon, Lydia. We have to get you some medical help."

"I'm all wet."

"We'll take care of that later. How do you feel?"

"I'm better. I think."

Her big eyes sent him a look that said they'd have to talk about things later. Much later. She was shaken by that kiss. And shocked, no doubt. It hadn't been the most proper thing to do—kiss his secretary. Or his administrative assistant, as Lydia liked to be called.

"Hurry," the gray-haired man said, urging them toward the door.

"How many?" Dev asked, glancing out the tiny bathroom window, his hands guiding Lydia forward.

"Four. They pulled up in a dark BMW, then fanned out."

"Did you recognize any of them?"

"No, dear boy, I'm afraid I didn't. If they're associated with CHAIM in any way, it's news to me. But they didn't stop for an introduction."

"Let's go," Dev said, giving his friend a nod that he was ready. "Lydia, hold on to my back and don't let go."

Lydia grasped his ruined jacket with a weak grip, as if she didn't have the strength to hold on. "Don't let go," he told her. He had to know she was right behind him at all times. "Got it?"

She nodded, her hands clutching the wet black wool, her eyes big with fear and fatigue.

"This way," the man said, guiding them out yet another door to a hallway. "This leads to the kitchen and then the yard beyond. Follow the hedge and stay in the shadows. There is a delivery truck waiting at the back entrance, right past the service gate. Get in it. I have people in place to hold them off, but only for a brief time."

"Who are you?" Lydia asked, lifting her head toward the man as Dev dragged her down the narrow hallway.

The man leading them smiled behind his mask. "Me? They call me The Peacemaker." He shot a glance at Dev. "I'm sure you've heard of me."

Dev nodded. He'd heard all right. They'd sent in a big gun to help him out of this mess. That could either be good or bad, depending on the outcome of this operation. And right now, that outcome didn't bode well for any of them.

"'Blessed be the peacemakers,'" Lydia said, her voice monotone and quiet. "'For they shall be called sons of God.'"

Dev prayed she wasn't going into shock. "I have to get her to a poison control center."

"You will have the proper help waiting in the truck," The Peacemaker assured him. "Kissie did her research and found an antidote to the pesticide, then she sent the truck to fetch you. The antidote is with the driver. Just get it into her system as quickly as you can."

They'd reached the butler's pantry leading into the long, modern kitchen. The Peacemaker checked to make sure no one was around. "I've distracted the caterers. You have just enough time to make a run for it." He opened the back door, then motioned them through.

Dev turned on the porch. "Who's really behind this?"

The Peacemaker looked down at the floor. "We're still not sure. But we're beginning to think it has something to do with the South American rescue that went bad a few years ago."

Dev let out a sigh. "The one Eli Trudeau—The Disciple—was involved in?"

"Yes. And we both know how that ended."

"But we still don't know if it's Eli, or someone else trying to get to me? We made a lot of enemies down there."

"Yes, we did. We'll keep searching until we have an answer, but everything we've found so far indicates The Disciple. We won't make a move until we're sure, of course. Meantime, you have your orders. I suggest you follow them to the letter."

Dev tugged Lydia close. "Eagle Rock."

"Hurry."

Dev looked back. "What about you?"

"Me? My dear boy, I was never here."

With that, The Peacemaker jumped off the porch and disappeared into the New Orleans night.

Lydia clung to Dev, then looked toward the shadowy path. "He never even took off his mask."

Dev didn't bother waving goodbye to The Peacemaker. They'd meet again before this was over, he was sure. He pulled Lydia away from the muted light coming from the crowded house. When he glanced back, he thought he saw something move just beyond the corner of the house.

"Lydia," he whispered close, "if I say run, you take off and don't look back."

"Will I turn into stone?" she quipped, but her voice sounded weak and shaky.

"Just don't look back. I mean it. Someone is following us."

Lydia moaned, but she kept moving. "What are you going to do?"

"I'm going to stop whoever it is. I want you near, but not harmed. If things go bad, you have to get to the truck and hope our man is inside. The code word is Eagle Rock. Do you understand?"

"Yes."

"Okay, here goes," Dev said, shoving her into a clump of hydrangea bushes, his body shielding hers. He waited, watching as the dark form crept along the shrubbery line. He had to take out the weapon first. With a practiced ease that surprised him since he'd been out of CHAIM for so long, Dev positioned himself in the shadows, then pounced hard, his foot lifting into a powerful kick toward the sleek handgun in the stranger's grasp.

The gun flew out into the air. The assailant grabbed his arm, then went into fight mode. Dev was ready with a second swift kick to the man's midsection, followed by a focused chop to his neck. The dark stranger fell into a clump by Dev's feet.

"Go," Dev whispered to Lydia, pushing her ahead of him. He glanced back once to make sure no other assailants were behind them. But The Peacemaker should have had a way of stopping assailants, and Dev figured his superior had taken care of the others by now.

Once they reached the dark alley, Dev turned to check on Lydia. "How are you?"

"Cold and wet," she said, pushing damp strands of hair off her face. "And I guess my makeup is ruined, huh?"

"You look fine," he told her. "But you're not out of the woods yet. We have to make sure the pesticides didn't get too far into your system."

"I'm not itching nearly as much now. But it's still hard to breathe."

"We'll take care of that." He gave her a quick hug, then turned to look up and down the alley for the truck. "There's our ride," he said, tugging Lydia by the arm. She had to hold on to the big towel to keep from tripping over it.

"I wish I had my Easy Spirits," she said. "These shoes are not made for quick getaways."

Glad her wry sense of humor was back, Dev looked down at her wet strappy high heels. "Just a few more steps. Once we get settled, we'll find dry clothes." He almost said "I promise" but then he remembered Lydia's heated words to him earlier.

And his to her. "No more promises."

He wouldn't promise her anything beyond each moment he could keep her alive. He'd just silently ask God to help him make that happen. *Please, Lord, help me. Keep her safe. Give her the promise of Your protection. Please.*

As they approached the big truck from behind, Dev held a finger to his lips, warning Lydia to stay quiet. He stood her beside the truck, then swiftly opened the driver's side door. "Where does the eagle dwell?" he asked the man he now had by the throat.

"It dwells on the rock," said the frightened man, "and resides on the crag of the rock and the stronghold."

"How do we get to the eagle?"

"Eagle's Rock, sir."

"We need to get out of here," Dev replied. Then he let the man go. "I'm The Pastoral."

"I've heard of you, sir," the young driver said. "I'm David. Nice to finally meet you."

"I wish we had time to chat," Dev replied, shaking the younger man's hand. Then he made a quick sweep of the shadows. "But I have to get this woman to safety."

"I understand. Climb into the back."

Dev nodded, then turned to Lydia. "Here, I'll help you up."

"Why the back?" she asked as he lifted her over the open flatbed with wooden, slitted panes on each side. "Wouldn't it be much nicer to ride inside with the driver?"

"Perhaps, but it would be much more dangerous."

Looking resigned, Lydia held her towel and dress and quickly climbed up onto the truck.

Dev hopped in after her, then glanced around. "Hay. Wonderful."

"And watermelons," Lydia said, the big towel held tightly around her. "I hope I don't start sneezing."

"You're allergic to watermelons?" he asked, hoping to at least lighten the moment a bit.

"No, silly. Hay." She grinned, then looked sad all over again.

Because of him, Dev thought. Because he'd brought her to this point.

"The hay and watermelons help to shield us from bullets," he explained. "We can hide back here much better than sitting up front. But if you're feeling worse—"

"I'll be all right," she said, her head down, her breath coming hard in spite of her efforts to be calm.

Dev hated the way she seemed to be slipping into defeat. He couldn't let Lydia give up. He hadn't. Not yet.

They sank into a corner near the cab of the big vehicle. Dev tugged her down, made sure she was covered, then knocked on the window.

The driver opened the panel. "Yes, sir?"

"Antidotes? Do you have any antidotes or a first-aid kit? I was told we'd have help for the poison in Miss Cantrell's system."

"Yes, sir," the young man said. He shoved a small package through the window. "We ran a research based on the information from Miss Kissie. There's an injection inside this pack."

"A shot?" Lydia said, sitting straight up against the wood-paneled truck. "I hate shots."

"I have to do this, Lydia," Dev told her. "To make you well."

"But I feel better now."

He hated the fear in her eyes. "But we have to be sure."

David cut his gaze toward the house. "And we need to hurry."

Dev quickly prepared the syringe, then looked over at Lydia. "I'll try to make it as painless as possible."

"Famous last words." But she held out her arm like a soldier about to be executed.

"I have to give it to you in your thigh," Dev explained, trying to sound calm.

Lydia let out a breath, then extended one of her legs. "Just get it over with, please."

Dev worked quickly and efficiently, thankful for the hours of training and fieldwork he'd had to school him for this. Lydia closed her eyes and let out a little groan as the needle penetrated her skin.

"How was that?" he asked as he pulled the damp towel back over her leg.

"I hardly felt a thing." But her eyes were still squeezed shut.

"You might become drowsy, but you'll be able to breathe much better soon." Dev tapped the window. "Let's get out of here."

David cranked the truck and they were off. The jostling caused Dev to fall toward Lydia, but as he tried to right himself, she reached out to grab his arm. "Stay close," she said. "Please?"

Her soft words were filled with a vulnerability that tore at his heart, and again, Dev felt the guilt of her fears washing over him. He had to take care of her, get her to a safe place. Then he'd find whoever was chasing them and take care of matters himself, if need be.

The way Eli did?

That question shot through his head like the glare of a rocket. Because of Lydia, Dev would have to be very careful to do things by the book.

So he scooted over to the corner and pulled her into his arms, holding her and making sure the damp towel had her covered for now. "Rest," he said into her ear. "Just rest."

He remembered telling her that the very first night they'd been on the run. Had that really been only a couple of days ago? As he held her, cushioning her with each bounce and shift of the big truck, he thought about how their relationship had gone from employee and employer to friends, and now, to something much more intimate and intense.

Now, they were two people on the run, forced together under extreme circumstances. And Dev had once again become the protector, because Lydia was dear to him and someone was trying to kill her. He'd keep running in order to save her.

Now, he'd breached all decorum and protocol and broken all the rules. He'd kissed her. And he wanted to kiss her again. But that couldn't happen.

He'd hurt her too many times already.

And how would Lydia feel when they reached

the end of the line? Would she still be his friend—his treasured friend—or would she hate him forever?

I'm hurting. How could he ever forget her angry face, the pain in her beautiful eyes, or those words she'd hurled at him? He never would forget. And he certainly couldn't forget that kiss they'd shared.

I'm hurting, too, Lydia, he thought now as he pulled her head down onto his chest. *I'm hurting for you, and for what might have been...for us.*

Lydia woke with a start, the smell of diesel fuel permeating her nose. Glancing around, she looked up into bright sunshine and Pastor Dev's haggard but handsome face. "Hello."

"Hello," he said, helping her to sit up. They were still in the back of the watermelon truck.

"Where are we?" she asked, squinting into the sun. The road was busy and multilaned, an interstate. Then she saw signs for Austin. "We're in Texas?"

"Yes, and we'll be at our destination soon." As if on cue, the truck turned off the interstate and headed down a long and winding county road. He gave her an appraising look. "How are you?"

Lydia knew she must look hideous with her smeared makeup and ratty hair. "I don't know. I need a mirror before I answer that question."

"You look better this morning. No rash or hives, and your pulse and breathing are both back to normal. I think the antidote did its job."

"I look like a drowned rat, and you know it."

He touched a hand to her temple in a gesture she was beginning to both love and hate. "You look beautiful to me, because you're not sick anymore." The fatigue in his eyes told her he'd kept vigil over her all night.

Feeling petty and contrite, she lowered her gaze. "Thank you, for saving my life."

He shrugged. "Part of the job."

That felt like a slap in the face, and just because she was weak and sore and dehydrated and hungry, she retorted. "And I guess that kiss was just part of the job, too, right?"

He had the good grace to look away. "That shouldn't have happened."

Her heart held the leftover fire of last night's rage. "Right."

"But…I had to calm you down."

"Well, that certainly did the trick, didn't it?"

"Lydia—"

"Don't," she said, holding up a hand and blinking back tears. "Don't try to explain or justify things. We're in deep trouble and…I know things are not as they seem. Even between us. Being chased, running for our lives, being thrown into such a chaotic situation, makes us do things we'd never do on a normal, routine day. Things such as kissing each other. Bad idea. So you need to understand, if…when we get out of this, I don't expect anything from you. Not one thing, except my old job back, of course. I do have bills to pay."

He actually managed a smile then, his eyes sweeping over her with regret and what looked a whole lot like longing. "We will get back to our old routine, Lydia. Somehow. And then, the worst thing we'll have to run from will be Mrs. Gordon's prune cake."

Lydia thought of ornery eighty-year-old Mrs. Gordon, bringing prune cake to each and every church function. Then she started giggling. Pastor Dev did, too. They both laughed so hard, tears were streaming down their faces when the truck came to an abrupt halt.

Lydia wiped at the tears, and wondered if they really were from laughing, or from a deep need to just sit and cry her eyes out. Maybe she was just too tired to think straight, but she thought the tears in Pastor Dev's eyes weren't from humor, either.

They both missed the life they'd left behind. Lydia's heart ached with all that had happened, all that he'd tried to save her from seeing. Not only did he have the burden of his friend's death back in Atlanta, but he had the burden of protecting her. And the memories of a past he'd tried to leave behind.

She couldn't stay mad at him. He was still a good man, still her hero, even if he did regret kissing her. She reminded herself that she wasn't supposed to complain, and she certainly wasn't supposed to take one little kiss seriously. One little, heart-changing, mind-altering kiss.

He gave her a long look filled with a dark intensity that scared her. She sent him a hopeful smile as a counteraction. "I'm okay. And right now, I'm so hungry, I'd even be willing to eat prune cake."

His eyes grew bright again, then he looked away

at the rich green pastures of the Texas hillside while he swiped at his face with his dirty jacket sleeve. And when he looked back, his eyes were dry. And blank.

NINE

Lydia relaxed in a luxurious robe, her face slathered in a mud mask, wondering how she'd gone from a drowned rat to reclining diva in a matter of minutes.

It was those women. The three with the big hair and the even bigger diamonds. Wishing she had her journal—which, along with Pastor Dev's trusty briefcase full of gadgets, had been left behind at Kissie's place—Lydia thought back over this morning's events, trying very hard *not* to think about that kiss that had started them on yet another grand adventure.

At least they were safe here in this country club retreat deep in the Texas hill country. After they'd gotten off the watermelon truck—and Lydia felt as if she'd fallen off the watermelon truck—Pastor Dev had turned her over to some of the richest matrons in Texas—or at least from the way they talked and acted, Lydia had surmised that. Then after telling her he'd see her later, he'd promptly disappeared to give a "briefing" to someone.

Lydia herself had been briefed on what to expect, but this briefing was more of a flutter of chatter and chuckles coming from her three matrons as they each introduced themselves and gave her a little bit of background.

"Hello, darlin', bless your heart." This from Lulu Anderson. Lulu had old oil money to burn, from everything Lydia could glean. And she had the bouffant blond hair and expensively altered skin to back it. "You just come with us, suga'. We're gonna get you all cleaned up and polished like a new set of pearls."

Lydia could only nod as she was ushered into a big, sprawling Spanish-style ranch house. The interior was light and open, with cool terra-cotta tiles and soft leather furniture everywhere. Out back, a large pool bubbled and flowed in never-ending serenity in front of a beautiful view of the distant hills and vistas. Servants hurried here and there, following Lulu's clipped, cultured instructions.

"We're putting Miss Lydia in the French suite," Lulu told an aging butler. "Hurry now, Alexandre."

"Don't worry about a thing, honey," Sally Mae Barton said, her black hair shimmering in its chignon. "We know how to handle these situations." Sally Mae reminded Lydia of an aging Scarlett O'Hara. And she seemed just as formidable.

"Are you all members of CHAIM?" Lydia, shocked and fatigued, asked.

"No, sweetie pie, not anymore. Now we're just married to men who are."

That caused Lydia's mind to venture into a territory she probably shouldn't be exploring at all. "So, CHAIM members are allowed to have families?"

"Sure, honey. Not only is it allowed, but it makes for a good cover." The third woman wrapped a plump arm around Lydia's shoulder. "I'm Rita Simpson. I'm an executive director with Mary Kay. You need a mask. Immediately."

"Of course she needs a mask, and a long nap, too," Lulu said, rolling her heavily lined blue eyes. "She'll get all of that, and yes, Rita, you can give her a makeover and some complimentary samples." She giggled. "Suga', this woman has made a fortune with Mary Kay. She's legendary around these parts."

"Do you drive a pink Cadillac?" Lydia asked, fascinated with these prim, overdressed, overperfumed women. Rita looked young in spite of her shimmering white, precisely clipped hair.

"Of course," Rita said with a dismissive shrug. "I'm on about my tenth one, I believe."

Remembering her first foray into being a diva in New Orleans, Lydia held up a hand. "I don't want anything too over the top. I just want to be clean and natural."

"We can do clean and natural," Rita said, her bright green eyes twinkling. "In fact, we have a whole line of products that'll give you the natural look."

Lydia wondered why she had to put on makeup to look natural, but she didn't argue. She was too dirty and tired to refuse the kindness of strangers, after all.

They stood Lydia in front of a massive, intricately carved door. Lulu gave the other two a wink, then said, "Now, Miss Lydia, this is your room. You're safe here. My husband, Alfred, hired the best security firm in Texas to make sure we are always safe here. If you open the door out onto the porch, an alarm will sound. So don't do that just yet, unless you have to escape right quick like. The Pastoral gave us strict orders to keep you inside unless he himself can escort you out for some fresh air. No one else. Just him. He wants to protect you. Do you understand, darlin'?"

Lydia did understand. She nodded, but couldn't manage to speak. She was just too tired to be mad at Pastor Dev's commando mode right now. "Thank you," she said.

"Let's pray," Lulu suggested, grabbing Lydia's hands in hers. The other women gathered in a protective circle around Lydia, then closed their eyes. Lydia stood silent as each one prayed for her safety.

"Lord, help our men find the ones behind this horrible situation. Bring them to a swift and fitting justice."

"And Lord, help this poor girl find some rest here in one of your safe pavilions. Protect our CHAIM warriors."

"Also, Lord, help us to help Lydia understand… about CHAIM and about…masks…and about men, too, I reckon."

"Amen." Lulu looked across at Rita. "Was that mask part really necessary?"

"I figured it couldn't hurt. A girl has to know how

to look her best in any situation—and she is under-cover."

With that, Lulu gave Lydia a quick hug. "Go on in. You'll be safe and you'll have complete privacy."

After the women brought her the softest robe she'd ever felt, Rita slapped something white and scented on her face, telling her to let it set for about ten minutes, then to rinse and pat her face gently.

"We'll send in some coffee and muffins for now, then we'll come back after your nap to get you up and ready for an early dinner out on the back patio."

"When will I see Pastor Dev again?" Lydia asked, wondering if she would ever see him. Had he abandoned her here, locked in a big, sprawling house with these matronly "What Not To Wear" experts?

Lulu glanced over to Sally Mae and Rita, her carefully etched eyebrows lifting. "You'll see him soon, honey. Meantime, we three might need to sit you down and explain what being in love with a CHAIM man involves."

Mortified, Lydia tried to hide her embarrassment. "But—"

Sally Mae patted her arm. "No buts about it, honey. We know love when we see it. After all, we've each been there. It's not easy to love a warrior, but it can be done."

"Does it show that much?" Lydia asked.

"Only when you take a breath," Rita replied, her eyes full of understanding.

Then the ladies had fluttered out like three butterflies, with waving hands and soft sighs and whispers.

So now here Lydia sat, on a brocade chaise lounge, with a mask drying over her features, wondering if Pastor Dev had a clue that she loved him. If everyone else could see it, why shouldn't he? Or maybe he did, and he was just ignoring it right now. But he'd kissed her as if he knew exactly how she felt.

"What am I to do, Lord?" she prayed out loud, her words echoing out over the high ceiling of the fancy gold-and-cream bathroom. "I've tried so hard to hide my feelings, but being on the run is getting to me. I love him so much, but I was in love with the man I knew. Now I don't even know him at all, and I still love him."

But, Lydia thought as she leaned her head back on the soft, scented pillow, her heart knew a real kiss from a necessary-for-the-circumstances kiss. And that kiss back in New Orleans had turned from necessary to much-needed before it had ended. He'd needed her. She'd felt it in the way his lips had touched on hers, in the way he'd held her close. In the way he'd taken care of her and held her all night in the watermelon truck.

A kiss in the shower, a ride in a watermelon truck. It was all too unbelievable, even for Lydia's romantic mind.

"He must think I'm a regular twit, a loose woman who'd throw herself at anyone, including her own boss and minister. What have I done, Lord? Why did I act so wanton and careless?"

Because you love him, came the reply. But Lydia

knew the reply hadn't come from God. That would be hers alone. Because she did love Pastor Dev. And she wished with all her heart he could return that love.

Sinking down into the fluffy pillows, she waited for an answer from above. But she heard only the silence of her gold-encased prison. And the beating of her own treacherous heart.

Dev stared across the table at the three men who'd brought him to Eagle Rock. Three distinguished, retired soldiers from CHAIM, men he'd admired and served with over the years. Men who now wanted the same answers he needed.

"I've told you everything I know," he said, worry and weariness causing him to sound harsh. "I know I was brought here for a reason. After all, it's not every day that a man gets invited to Eagle Rock."

Eagle Rock meant even more big guns had become involved.

Alfred Anderson leaned forward, his craggy face etched in a frown. In a deep Texas drawl, he said, "Pastoral, we know it's been hard, being thrown back into the thick of things. But we can't keep holding them off, and you can't keep running—it's like squatting with your spurs on. We gotta find out who's behind these attacks and end this thing, once and for all."

Dev knew what that meant. "But we've never attacked one of our own. And we still don't have proof that The Disciple is behind this."

Gerald Barton got up to pour himself another glass of iced tea, then he stood, tall and big-chested, his crystal glass in his hand. "But all indications lead to him. He swore he'd get even with all of us whenever he got out of the retreat."

"The prison, you mean," Dev countered. "We sent him to a locked, carefully watched facility. Eli knew what we were doing. Call it a spiritual retreat, but we locked the man away."

"We had no other choice," John Simpson said, anger coloring his words to match his ruddy complexion. "Eli was getting too bold, too careless. And we still don't have all the clear details of what happened in South America. For all we know, his actions were what caused this tragedy."

Dev hit a hand on the marble-topped table centered in the dark paneled library. "I turned the man in, John. I was the whistle-blower who caused Eli to lose his family. And for that, I can never forgive myself. I don't really blame him for coming after me. I deserve whatever he wants to do to me."

"You don't deserve to die," Alfred retorted, "and that young woman certainly doesn't deserve any of this."

Dev sank back in the oxblood leather chair. "No, Lydia is an innocent victim. And she's the only reason I haven't taken matters into my own hands."

"Don't be foolish, son," Alfred said, a hand up. "You know what going off on a vigilante quest did to Eli. You're too good a man to let that happen to you."

"But I can't bear it if Lydia becomes collateral

damage. If…" He closed his eyes to the fatigue draining him. "I just couldn't bear that."

"Then there's only one thing to do," John said. "We have to draw Eli out, get the truth out of him. Whatever it takes, you need to meet with him face-to-face."

"How can we make that happen?"

Gerald leaned forward. "Let's review the situation, then go from there. We have to be sure. CHAIM is not in the mercenary business. We try to save people, not take them out. Harm none. That's why we brought you here. To give you time to think clearly."

Dev got the meaning of that statement. He was being ordered to chill out. "I'm clear on everything, gentlemen. Especially the fact that someone is out to get me. As angry as Eli was and probably still is, he was…he is my friend. I can't believe he'd do this to me, to this organization. It just doesn't add up."

"But Eli has possibly compromised our entire operation," John replied, frowning. "You yourself said he blames you for turning him in before he could go after those people down in South America. It might come down to you or him, Devon."

"I won't kill him," Dev said, his tone brooking no argument. He'd die himself before he'd take another human being's life. Especially that of his friend and fellow team member.

"Did your assailant in Atlanta leave any clues at all?" Gerald asked, turning to Dev.

"Nothing that I know of," Dev replied. He lifted

a thick file from the table. "We've all read over the official CHAIM report. Our operative in the Atlanta police department was careful to make sure we received a detailed CSI report. It was a clean crime. No prints, no weapons found. They used a silencer, and they got out quickly."

"Then they realized their mistake," John added. "And that's why someone is still out there, trying to kill you."

"Eli wouldn't do that. He wouldn't send someone else."

"He's changed, Dev." Gerald shrugged. "It happens. Eli was a good man in training, but his faith was always shaky. He might not pull the trigger, but he could order it done."

Alfred nodded. "He only joined CHAIM to please his father. I don't think his heart was ever in it."

Dev nodded. No one knew who Eli's father was, and Eli refused to ever talk about him. But the man had been a high-ranking official in the CHAIM link, until he'd been killed many years ago, somewhere in Africa. That had been the saving grace in Eli's enforced seclusion and recovery. Out of respect for his father, and his loss, their superiors had been lenient and forgiving with Eli.

"Maybe Eli joined for all the wrong reasons, but then he lost his wife and unborn child, because of us," Dev reminded them. "Because of me."

"Or because of his own hotheaded carelessness," John countered. "We just don't know."

Dev ran a hand down his unshaven face. "My gut

tells me that there's something more to this. And I can't help but think it still involves the cartel we infiltrated in South America. It stands to reason that if Eli is out, the cartel leaders might be after him. And maybe they came to Atlanta hoping to send us a warning."

"By killing you?" Gerald shook his head. "I doubt that. Why wouldn't they just find Eli and end it once and for all?"

"Because Eli knows how to hide," Dev said. "What better way to bring him out of hiding than by killing a team member and a friend—a former friend whom he now considers to be an enemy?"

"You have a point," John said. "If Eli thought you'd been killed, he might go after the cartel again. Either to avenge your death and that of his family, or to join up with them as a reward."

"And the glaring problem is," Alfred added, "we don't know which way Eli has turned. He might be back in the fold, or he might be lost to us forever."

Dev got up and walked to the big window that gave a stunning view of the hill country surrounding the secluded hideaway. "Then we have to keep searching. We need to put out more encryptions, see if we get anyone's attention. If Eli is in danger and if he wants our help, he'll answer us."

Alfred turned to the command system set up on his antique teakwood desk. "Then let's get to it." He keyed in a message, then turned to face the others. "Each guest room here is equipped with laptops— cleared for use by CHAIM members only. Check yours when you retire to your rooms. All we can do for now is watch and wait."

"And pray," Gerald replied.

Dev stayed by the window, his thoughts on Lydia. Her safety was his main concern right now. If Eli had turned rogue, he wouldn't stop at just getting even. He might kill Lydia, just to get to Dev. But if Eli was in trouble, if someone from South America was after the entire CHAIM team, then they would do worse damage, far worse damage, than Eli ever thought about. Because these men were the very essence of evil.

And he shuddered to think what they would do to an innocent young woman.

Lydia woke to late-afternoon sunshine streaming into her room. Rubbing her eyes, she longed for her own bed back in Dixon. Even though this white-wood, elegant sleigh bed with the beautiful peach silk comforter and sheets was lovely, Lydia felt strange being encased in so much luxury.

"My mama would flip her lid," Lydia said to herself, her voice sounding scratchy and husky.

She got up, determined to try and salvage what little decency she had left. She felt so out of sorts, dressing up in fancy evening clothes, kissing a man in the shower, sleeping the day away. This wasn't Lydia's style. She was used to hard work and a strong moral fiber. Not silk sheets and sparkly dresses.

But everyone she'd met on this strange trip had

been kind and devoted. All believers, even if they did march to the beat of a different drummer.

"Are You trying to teach me something, Lord?" she asked as she hurried to the big wardrobe across the room. Rita had told her she'd find clothes inside. "Are You showing little sheltered, protected, narrow-minded Lydia Cantrell that the world is made up of all kinds of Christians?"

The silence of the still summer day echoed out over her head. "Okay, maybe You've just abandoned me all together."

She instantly regretted thinking that way and said a quick prayer for forgiveness. God had not abandoned her. He'd been right there, helping Pastor Dev to protect her. And being alive on this nice summer day was proof of that.

"I'm going to shut up and get dressed," Lydia told herself and God. She found a nice floral T-shirt and some denim capris in her size, wondering how everyone knew how to dress her. At least she was learning important wardrobe tips, if nothing else.

She'd just started combing her hair when she heard a knock at the door. "Who is it?"

"It's Alexandre, ma'am. I'm to bring you to the dining room. Casual dress is fine."

"I'll be right there," Lydia replied to the butler, thinking casual was more to her liking. Looking in the bottom of the wardrobe, she found some pink leather flip-flops. They matched the flowers in her shirt, so she put them on and found they to fit. "Close enough."

But before she could reach the door, it swung

open. In pranced Rita and Sally Mae, all smiles and floral scents.

"You can't possibly go to dinner without proper makeup," Rita said, slapping her Mary Kay case down on the bed. "We sent Alexandre away. Honestly, that man is the most uppity butler I've ever seen. He didn't want to let us in. Sit down over here, honey, and let us work on you a little bit."

"I don't want much makeup," Lydia replied. But she sank down on the soft cream-colored stool in front of the elaborate French provincial vanity. "I just need a little blush and gloss. You know, Kissie fixed me up in New Orleans and it was just a tad too much."

"We understand," Sally Mae said, smiling at Lydia's reflection in the mirror. "You don't want to paint the barn door too red, right?"

Lydia nodded, confused. "Right." Then she pivoted. "Is Kissie okay?"

"She's fine. The girl who tattled has been taken care of—sent to a rehab center."

Lydia sighed. "I'm glad Kissie is all right. I liked her, even if she did dress me in slinky red."

"We won't overdo it, but you don't want to look like you've been rode hard and put up wet," Rita said, then grinned at Lydia's shocked expression. "Like an old mare that's been on a long gallop."

"Oh." Lydia shook her head. "I don't want to look like an old mare, that's for sure."

"You will look just right," Rita said, one diamond-heavy finger posed on her face as she analyzed

Lydia's skin. "Nice complexion. So creamy and with just a touch of cute freckles. And that hair—it's to die for."

"Well, someone has been trying to kill me," Lydia quipped.

"She has the right attitude," Sally Mae said, her diamond tennis bracelet winking at Lydia. "When you love a CHAIM man, you have to have a sense of humor."

"How did y'all do it?" Lydia asked, curious and hoping to gain some pointers. "How'd y'all meet your husbands?"

Rita chuckled as she plucked Lydia's eyebrows. "I sold Mary Kay to John's mother and sisters. They set us up, but of course, he balked. CHAIM men have a definite commitment problem, being as they are always out saving the world and all that." She shrugged. "But I didn't give up. I just bided my time and waited for him to come home. Then I pounced on the man and told him I loved him and wanted to spend the rest of my life with him. He was so overwhelmed, he said yes right away. That was thirty-five years and three children ago. I've prayed many a night for him to come home safe. Now he's retired and I'm as tickled as a pig in a mud puddle."

Lydia laughed, then turned to Sally Mae. "Your turn."

"I was a CHAIM operative," Sally Mae explained, grinning. "Met Gerald in London. It was during the late seventies and we were in place to watch some really aggressive cult members who'd snatched a young American girl. I posed as a free-spirited girl and infiltrated this rather nasty cult. He was my contact person on the outside. It wasn't love at first sight. He had to chase me until I let him catch me. Been letting him chase me for over thirty years now."

Lydia was amazed that petite, spry Sally Mae with the long, perfectly manicured pink fingernails and matching toes had been an undercover operative. "That must have been some adventure."

"It was. We saved a lot of Christians from terrible things. And CHAIM still does that."

"These are hard times," Rita added, her fingers buffing and blending Lydia's eyes and face. "World terror, countries in chaos, and the innocents who get caught in the fray. Our men are very special to us, but when called to duty, they have to go."

"For the greater good," Lydia said, her eyes going wide as she stared at them in the mirror.

"For the greater good," Sally Mae repeated. "I see you've heard some of the rules already."

"More than I ever wanted to know," Lydia said.

"It's all about serving the Lord," Rita said, her hand holding Lydia by the chin while she painted gloss on Lydia's lips. "These men are trained to help Christians the world over. But sometimes, it's all about loving your man so much it hurts."

"I do," Lydia admitted, the pain of that admission searing her heart. "I loved him when I didn't know about any of this, and I think I love him even more now. But I don't think he's even aware of it. He was barely aware I was even alive until someone tried to kill both of us."

"Oh, he's aware, all right."

They all turned as Lulu came clicking into the room, a soft smile on her face. "In fact, I feel pretty sure that if we don't get you out there to dinner soon, the man will come charging in here and throw you over his shoulder, the way Alfred did me when I refused to elope with him thirty-six years ago. I was a debutante and sorority girl and he was a hard-edged wildcatter, but mercy, I didn't want to admit that I loved him. So he kinda took matters into his own hands."

Stunned, Lydia said, "Oh, Pastor Dev would never—"

Just then, there was a pounding on the door. "Lydia, are you in there? Is everything all right?"

It was Pastor Dev.

"I'm coming," Lydia called. "I'm fine, just running a little behind."

"Well, hurry up. I was worried sick."

"I rest my case," Lulu said, a knowing smile on her face. "Now, suga', let's get out there and have a nice evening with our menfolks."

"But…I need to know how to do that," Lydia whispered. "I mean, I need to know how to love such a complicated man."

Rita finished, then rubbed her hands together. "Oh, that's easy, honey. Just keep smiling and praying. No matter how much your poor heart is breaking."

"For the greater good?"

"For that, and your own sanity."

TEN

Lydia woke with a start.

Someone was in her room. She couldn't make out any human shapes since it was raining heavily and there was no moonlight. But she could feel the presence in the big wide bedroom.

And she could hear her own fast breathing.

She pulled the covers up to ward off her fears. "Who's there?"

Nothing.

The rain fell in a continuous drone, muffling any noise that might seem different. When had the storm approached? And how had she slept through that and someone entering her room? Maybe she'd just been dreaming.

Just to be safe, Lydia searched for the phone on the bedside table. There was a red button for emergencies. Lulu had shown it to her and stressed that she should touch it if she felt in danger.

She reached for the button, but a strong arm pushed her hand away. Her breath caught and a cold wave of fear rushed through her system. She tried to speak, but no words would come.

"I wouldn't call anyone just yet."

"Alexandre?" She recognized the cultured voice of the butler. She almost wanted to giggle—they could actually say the butler did it. But she couldn't muster even a scared chuckle. She swallowed, prayed, tried to think. Tried to stall him. "Alexandre, is everything all right?"

"No," the man holding her said. "Everything is not all right. You're a very pretty woman, but you know too much. You've seen too much. I hate to do this... but beware the wolf in sheep's clothing."

Lydia watched as he raised a pillow in the air, and she knew right then that she would die if she didn't do something quick to help herself. If she could just make it to the French doors and then the porch, she could trip the alarm system. She had to do something, right now.

In his room across the hall, Dev sat skimming his e-mails. He couldn't sleep, so he'd decided to give it one last shot. Blurry-eyed, he blinked as the screen flashed white and alive before him. Then he saw it— an instant message popped up on the screen.

The black sheep has no shepherd. He has no master. He is scattered on the mountain.

Dev sat up in his chair, his mind humming, his heart racing. Eli?

The Disciple had a mountain retreat in Colorado, and he'd always joked that he was the black sheep of their particular team. Was Eli trying to tell Dev something?

Dev typed.

'What do you understand that is not us?'

Eli would know to look to Job. He'd know the verse and understand the code. What do you know?

The answer came quickly.

'Both the gray-haired and the aged are among us.' Hide anything received.

Not "Do not hide" like the original verse from Job. But "hide." Eli wanted Dev to withhold information? That could be a trick, or it could be a warning. Did Eli know something that would help them both?

His pulse pounding, Dev typed,

'What shall I answer you?'

The response came back. The black sheep has no shepherd. Then no more codes, but an outright denial.

I didn't do it, Pastoral. It's a setup. Beware the gray-haired man. Don't walk with the wicked men.

Then Eli was gone, leaving Dev to stare at the words frozen on the screen. Eli had broken procedure to speak bluntly, which meant he, too, was on the run. Dev could only hope no one else had intercepted the message. But who? What was Eli saying? He'd repeated part of the message Kissie had sent earlier, so Dev knew Eli was keeping tabs on them. But what was he trying to say?

Dev thought back—what gray-haired man? Did Eli mean the man dressed as a granny woman back in Atlanta? Or the three men who were now helping Dev? They all had a tinge of gray in their hair. But even that description could be some sort of coded warning. Who else had helped Lydia and him? Kissie? No one in her charge had gray hair.

Then it hit him as though doused by the rain outside.

The Peacemaker. He certainly was a distinguished-looking, gray-haired man. And because of the mask, Dev had never actually seen his face.

Was Eli trying to warn him that The Peacemaker was behind this? But that didn't make sense. The Peacemaker had purposely helped Dev and Lydia in New Orleans. Thinking back over it, Dev realized The Peacemaker had been the one to send him here to Eagle Rock. He'd also been the one to give Dev a message from Kissie. And that message had saved Lydia's life. So how could he be involved, other than trying to help?

But…Dev hadn't confirmed that message. He hadn't spoken to Kissie again since coming here. He'd only talked to her about the poisoning and how to stop it. Grabbing his Treo, he immediately dialed Kissie's private number.

She didn't answer. And he didn't dare leave a message.

Dev got up and ran a hand through his hair. The rain picked up, the wind howling around the long, rambling house. He heard something bang, then he heard what sounded like a scream. The next thing he heard was the alarm.

Lydia!

Dev dashed across the hall to Lydia's room, his fists banging hard against the door. "Lydia?" The door was locked, so he quickly stepped back, aiming his entire body against the heavy wood. The door-jamb shattered even as his shoulder throbbed with a white-hot pain, but he was inside and running before he even registered that.

"Lydia?" He called her name over and over as he raced to hit the light switch. When he turned on the overhead light, he saw the crumpled form of Alexandre near the night table, a shattered lamp pedestal lying nearby, and the patio doors wide open. Then he saw Lydia standing out in the middle of the yard, rain washing over her.

And she was screaming.

Lydia hadn't known what else to do. She'd received an e-mail long ago with self-defense tips for women. She'd memorized it. And boy, had those tips come in handy tonight.

First, she'd managed to use her own trapped arm for leverage, yanking with all her might so she could land a kick in his midsection. That had caused Alexandre, the so-called butler, to scream out in pain. Then she'd used her free elbow to jab him in the face and her fingers to poke at his eyes. He crumpled away from her. Since his only weapon was a pillow, Lydia could only imagine that he'd planned to smother her, asleep or awake. She wasn't about to let that happen.

While Alexandre held his hands to his eyes, Lydia, working on pure adrenaline, hit him over the head with the crystal lamp on the side table, and ran for the doors, opening them wide, welcoming the blaring sound of the security alarm.

The rain felt good on her fevered skin, the wind cold on her heated face. She remembered to scream as loud as she could. And she was still screaming when Pastor Dev grabbed her up in his arms and pulled her back to the long porch.

"Lydia," he said, his hands on her hair. "Lydia, are you all right?"

She stopped screaming, her breath coming in big gulps now. "I'm fine. Just mad, is all. The butler tried to kill me. How stupid is that?"

The look in his eyes—part terror, part admiration—told her that he did care about her. And that gave her a sense of calm. Gulping a deep breath, she said, "I'm all right, really."

"Thank You, God," Pastor Dev said, lifting up the prayer to the heavens. Then he pulled Lydia into his arms and held her close. "I'm so sorry. I was supposed to be watching out for you."

"I'm all right," Lydia kept telling him. "I…I remembered…somehow I remembered my self-defense tips."

He pulled back to stare down at her. "You sure did. Alexandre looks pretty beat-up."

"He made me mad," she retorted. "I'm just so tired of people trying to kill me. They act nice, then they turn nasty. It's just not right."

Pastor Dev planted a kiss on her wet forehead. "Let's get you inside."

"Do you know that every time you kiss me, I'm all wet?" Lydia asked. "It's not very romantic." Then she held a hand to her mouth. "Oh, never mind. I mean…forget I said that. You were just being kind."

He didn't answer. Instead he just stood there looking at her, his dark eyes as bright and shimmering as the rainwater falling off the tiled roof. "Lydia, I—"

They were interrupted by a herd of Eagle Rock dwellers coming out onto the porch. Lulu had on a white satin robe, her hair still just as big and perfect as it had been all day. "Mercy, what in the world happened in there?"

Alfred was right behind her, the few hairs he had on his head standing straight up. "Alexandre is hurt."

"Alexandre tried to harm Lydia," Pastor Dev replied. "I hope he's more than hurt. Don't let him get away."

Alfred shouted back into the room. "Detain the butler."

"My Alexandre?" Lulu asked, her hands on her hips. "But…that just doesn't make sense."

"Nothing does right now, darlin'," her husband

said. "This is worse than a bee after a bull. We can't trust anyone."

"Alexandre?" Sally Mae stood just inside the open doors, her hair down now and hanging in waves to her waist. "I can't believe it. We did a thorough background check on that man."

"He's only worked for us a few months," Lulu pointed out. Then she gasped. "He was planted here, wasn't he, Alfred?"

"Apparently," Alfred said, his gaze sweeping over the others. "We have to be more careful. I'll have to have a meeting with the other employees and explain what happens when someone is disloyal."

Lydia didn't dare ask about that. She tried to remember that CHAIM didn't want to do harm, but anyone would do harm to protect their loved ones, wouldn't they? Even this Disciple person everyone was talking about.

That made her remember something Alexandre had said while he held her down. "Alexandre told me to beware the wolf in sheep's clothing. Do you think he was talking about The Disciple?"

Pastor Dev looked at John and Alfred. "I've had a message from The Disciple."

Alfred nodded, his expression taut. "Why don't we get you two dry then meet in the kitchen. You can fill us in."

"I won't meet without Lydia. I'm not leaving her alone again."

John nodded. "Lydia can be trusted."

Lydia beamed in spite of being so scared. She'd

rather be in the thick of things than resting comfortably in a room where she'd almost been smothered. "I'll go get changed."

Lulu guided her back inside. "You remembered to open the doors to set the alarm off. Smart, honey, real smart."

"I can take care of myself," Lydia replied. But she gave the still-moaning Alexandre, who was being held down by Gerald and the very strong-armed Rita—who looked stunning even without all her Mary Kay—a very wide berth. Lydia did not want to have to kick Alexandre back down. But she would. She'd had just about enough.

Everyone left, Gerald dragging Alexandre out. Pastor Dev turned at the door, facing Lydia and Lulu. "I'll wait right outside."

"I'll get her dressed," Lulu said, patting his arm. "I'll make sure—"

Pastor Dev didn't let her finish. Pushing back inside, he asked, "Are you sure you're all right, Lydia?"

Lydia nodded. "I'm okay. I'm fine. I'm not going into shock and I'm not going to fall apart. I just want this to be over."

Lulu shot a worried look at Pastor Dev. "Maybe I should give the two of you some privacy."

"Good idea," Pastor Dev said, his eyes on Lydia.

Lulu nodded. "Coffee. We need coffee. And I don't need a butler to make that." Then she added, "You have five minutes before I come back." She left, but not before giving them a long, meaningful glance over her shoulder.

Lydia waited while Pastor Dev stood in the open doorway. Not wanting to add to his burdens, she said, "I'll be fine, honestly." Then she saw him wince and grab his right shoulder. Unable to stop herself, she touched her fingers to his mighty biceps. "You're hurt!"

"It's nothing," he said, eyeing the splintered door frame. "I ran into the door."

"You broke the door down," Lydia said, observation style.

"I broke the door down," he replied, commando style.

"You did that, for me?"

"I...was afraid—"

"I told you, I'm fine."

"Lydia," he began. Then he stopped, let out a frustrated sigh and pulled her into his arms. This time, he didn't kiss her to calm her down, or to shut her up. This time, Lydia had no doubt that he was kissing her because he wanted to.

So she kissed him back, wanting this, too.

The room was quiet, the only sound the rain now coming soft and gentle outside the house. That and Lydia's contented sigh as the man she loved showed her with tenderness what he couldn't say with words.

He loved her, too. A little bit at least.

Dev stared across the table, trying to look anywhere but into Lydia's big, questioning eyes. It had been so hard, earlier, to let her go, to stop holding her, to stop kissing her. But he'd somehow managed to pull away, to push her back into her room and urge her to change out of her wet pajamas.

He couldn't allow his feelings for Lydia to side-track him. Someone was out to do him in and he was beginning to think that *someone* was much closer than he had imagined. His gut told him to believe Eli's warning.

Which meant he had to keep Lydia close, but he also had to keep her at arm's length. He had hoped to leave her at Eagle Rock, safe and sound, while he finished this job. But now he couldn't do that. Now he had to take her with him. Just until this was over. And he could only wonder what their lives would be like if and when this were ever truly over.

"Here, Pastoral, drink this." Lulu handed him a large glass of orange juice and two pain pills. "You look like you need it. Your arm is bruised."

He didn't miss the meaning in her eyes. Her expression held the same warning look Kissie had given him in New Orleans the night he'd first seen Lydia in the red dress. Lulu Anderson was a wise woman. She knew more than just his arm was bruised.

He had to hold it all together. "Thanks," he said, taking the juice from Lulu. He tossed back the pills, then drank the juice, his eyes closed. When he opened them, Lydia was still staring over at him.

They were all up now and Lulu was cooking an early-morning breakfast of blueberry pancakes and bacon. The aroma of the sweet pancakes merged with the tantalizing smell of crisp bacon. Dev wasn't hungry.

Gerald leaned forward, drumming his fingers on the long cypress-planked breakfast table. "What do you think Eli's message means?"

Dev hadn't given them the complete message, so he looked down at his hands. "I think he's trying to warn me. He said he didn't do it. I believe him."

"But…who then?" John asked, glancing around the full table. "Eli could be trying to throw you off, Devon."

Alfred poured himself another cup of coffee and sat down by Lydia. "Alexandre isn't talking…yet. But he has implied that he's been in contact with The Disciple. Maybe that's who he got his orders from, too."

That caught Dev's attention. "What did he say?"

"He would only tell us that The Disciple is out there and he's after the people who wronged him."

"And how does Alexandre know this?" John asked, his expression skeptical.

"Well, he did mention a wolf in sheep's clothing," Gerald reminded Dev. "That certainly sounds like Eli."

"Or maybe Alexandre was just trying to finger Eli," Dev retorted, trying to gauge the body language around the table. Were they all evading him? Did John's fisted hand mean he was preparing for a fight? Why wouldn't Gerald look Dev in the eye? And Alfred was as fidgety as a mad rooster. Did they all know something Dev needed to know?

Dev had never had any doubts about trusting the other CHAIM operatives. But now, he had to wonder if one or all of the men at this table were behind this whole sordid affair. Was someone inside CHAIM somehow connected to the drug cartel they'd busted up a few years ago? Had that same someone ordered the executions of Eli's wife and unborn child?

It couldn't be possible.

And what about The Peacemaker? Dev had never worked with the legendary agent, but the man was well-known in the secret CHAIM brotherhood. Well-known, but not really accessible. No one even knew the man's real name. He was that elusive, that deep undercover. And yet, many successful rescue and recover missions had come under the leadership of The Peacemaker. Was he the wolf in sheep's clothing?

Gerald's words brought Dev out of his musings. "Alexandre pledges that he only wanted to scare Lydia, that he was ordered by someone very high up to scare the girl so that Dev would take her and leave."

Dev got up, then looked around the table. "Well, that's exactly what I'm going to do. I am going to take Lydia and leave. Only this time, I'm not telling anyone where we're going."

"You can't do that, son," Gerald retorted, shocked. "You know the rules. Operatives have to report in on a daily basis."

"I'm changing the rules," Dev told them. "And you'd all be wise to stay out of it. I don't want any of you blamed for a decision I'm making on my own."

"Why are you doing this?" Lulu asked, her hand on his arm.

"Because every time I think Lydia's safe, someone else comes along to put her in danger. She
wasn't safe in New Orleans and she isn't safe here.
The fewer people involved, the better. I won't put
any of you in jeopardy."

Alfred nodded, then held up a hand when the
others sat up to protest. "He has a point, gentlemen.
Sometimes, in the thick of things, we have to make
tough decisions. We've all been there. And right now,
Devon is thinking he can't entirely trust us. Am I
right, Pastoral?"

Dev didn't even blink. Let them sweat. "You are,
sir. So I hope you'll understand why I have to do my
job. I have to protect Lydia."

Sally Mae nodded, then patted her chignon. "I
certainly remember those days—having to do what
we knew was right. The Pastoral can give a thorough
report when this is settled and over."

"It's the VEPs," Lydia said, her quiet voice
echoing out over the room.

"Excuse me?" Lulu asked, frowning.

"Very Evil People," Lydia replied. "Someone very
evil is behind this. And none of y'all look evil." She
shrugged. "But I've been wrong before."

"Oh, like VIPs, but different," Sally Mae said,
nodding. "It's not us, honey. I stand by that." She
looked around as if to verify her words.

"I'd like to believe that," Lydia replied. She
looked shaken, but she held up her chin. "Pastor Dev
will find them, whoever they are. I know that."

"Then we should do everything in our power to

make that happen," Alfred said, nodding toward Dev. "But going off on your own—that dog don't hunt, Devon. We need to work together."

"Yes, together," the others echoed, their sincerity reeking of a setup in Dev's paranoid mind.

They all agreed so easily, Dev noted, watching for any signs of deception. But it was hard to see anything. These men were old pros, which made it nearly impossible to access their real motives. Even their wives wore blank expressions that revealed nothing.

"Why was I summoned here?" Dev asked, giving each of them a direct look. "I need to know that before I go anywhere, or before I agree to anything else."

Alfred let out a sigh. "Pastoral, we've been behind you since you left Atlanta. You did the right thing, going to Kissie. She got the message out to The Disciple and now he's responded."

"Yes, that's the good news," Dev said. "But how in the world did someone get to that girl in New Orleans? How did we allow Lydia to be contaminated with a dangerous pesticide?"

"Someone is watching and working from the inside," John said, his expression open and sincere. "We just have to find out who the mole is. There are many who want us to fail. Someone is passing on inside information, hoping to bring down this organization."

"And that information brought danger right to our door again," Dev said. "I thought this was a safe haven for Lydia. But the butler? It even sounds cliché to me and I've seen it all."

"We brought you both here because we thought we could protect you and help you find our enemies, and we needed to stall you for a while," Alfred said. "This place is a stronghold. Alexandre was a blunder. Someone set him up with the best of credentials, knowing that a lot of our agents pass through here."

"How did that someone know to do that? How did that someone know I'd wind up at Eagle Rock?"

John hit a hand on the table. "Because it's standard procedure to bring an agent in trouble here," he said, his eyes going wide. "You know that, Devon. We brought Eli here when he…when things went bad for him. This is the resting place for agents who need a time-out."

"So Alexandre just happened to be in the right place at the right time?" Dev asked as he leaned forward. "Exactly when I was brought here for a…time-out."

"I'm afraid so," Alfred replied. "Good help is hard to find."

"We're sorry we let you down, son," John said. "We're still trying to locate The Disciple and we're still investigating all of these actions, but you're free to go—as long as you do things by the book. We'll get to the bottom of this. In the meantime, how can we help you?"

Dev glanced at Lydia, then motioned for her to get up. "Well, you can loan me a means of transportation."

"Of course," Gerald said. "We have all sorts of vehicles."

"I don't need a vehicle," Dev said. "I need a plane. Lydia and I are going to fly out of here. And none of you will know where we're going."

"You can't—"

"I can and I will," Dev shot back, his glaring gaze stopping Gerald in midsentence. "Don't make me do this the hard way. Just let us leave."

"What about the pilot?" John asked. "He'll need a flight plan."

"I'll be the pilot," Dev replied. "And let's just say, I'm going to fly under the radar."

"I don't like this, not one little bit," Alfred said, getting up to stare across the table at Dev. "Son, you need to think this through."

"I have thought it through," Dev replied, his hand on Lydia's arm. "Since I can't trust anyone right now, I have to do things my way. And that means getting out of here."

"We'll have to report this," John said, his expression grim.

"I'd expect no less," Dev replied. "And I'll accept responsibility for my actions."

Sally Mae looked around the room, then she sent her husband a pleading look. "Let them go, John. We have to trust Dev's decision and his instincts."

Dev nodded. "Good point. But I'm only worried about one person's opinion right now." He looked at Lydia. "Do *you* trust me?"

She stood silent, her eyes speaking volumes as they went from bright and luminous to frightened and unsure. But behind her ever-changing gaze, Dev saw the spirit and spunk he'd come to admire. Lydia was one of the bravest women he'd ever known.

She gave him a slight nod. Then she stood closer to him, smiled at everyone in the room, looked back over at him and said, "When do we leave?"

ELEVEN

Pastor Dev turned to Lydia. "All buckled in?"

She nodded, then glanced at what looked like television screens in front of them on the instrument panel. "Are you really going to fly this plane?"

"I'm trained to fly this plane."

She was still in awe. People with power sure could get things done in a real hurry. "I can't believe they let you go so easily—and gave you a private Cessna to boot."

He was in full commando mode again, checking the controls with the precision of an astronaut. "Oh, that was just a front, sweetheart. They'll send someone to monitor us—no doubt on that." Then he grinned. "If they can find us, that is. But this isn't just any old Cessna. This is a sweet Skyhawk SP, top-of-the-line. A very intelligent plane. This instrument panel is cutting edge—a G1000—"

"I'm glad you're so happy with our new ride," Lydia interrupted. "But I'm a wee bit concerned that we might be shot down in midair."

He sent her a reassuring glance then nodded toward the little flat screens. "I'm not worried about that, not with this high-tech setup. Great situational, real-time awareness with both this PDF and MFD— that's primary flight display and multifunction display in laymen's terms. Even if they come after us, this baby will make a clean getaway. This is a go-fast plane as long as we fly her under 14,000. She gets a little antsy in dense altitude." He actually winked at her, then gave her a Bogart kind of smile. "Sweetheart."

Lydia let his uncharacteristic excitement and technotalk roll right over her, noting that this was the most the man had ever spoken to her, outside of preaching a sermon, of course. She thought about mentioning that he'd been calling her *sweetheart* an awful lot lately, but she refrained from that. Why spoil a perfectly good getaway moment with mushy stuff?

"So they let you go just to save face?"

"Something like that. As I've told you, CHAIM is not a violent organization. More like passive persuasion."

"Oh, right. VEPs use the old-fashioned, killing kinds of persuasion, but y'all are just ever so friendly and accommodating. Do you really expect me to believe that?"

"We only resort to brute force when necessary— like when the man at the train station tried to gun us down—he was carrying a lethal weapon. I had to maim him, to stop him from killing you. The same with Alexandre. He's being taken care of—but he won't be harmed. He'll just live to regret what he did."

A shudder went down Lydia's spine as she imagined Alexandre stuck in a padded room, having to learn the books of the Bible…or else. Of course, that would serve him right for trying to put a pillow over her face. "You say that with such ease. Doesn't all this trickery and double-crossing stuff get to you after a while?"

He stopped fidgeting with the instrument panel, his hands going still on the controls. His expression told her that after enjoying a brief reprieve with the distraction of this sleek cockpit, he was now back to reality. "It did get to me. That's why I retired. That's why I wish you weren't involved."

Lydia could see the torment in his eyes. Wishing she could take back her question, she asked him another one instead. "Why do they call you The Pastoral?"

He gave her a wry smile. "I got that name in training school. Eli and some of the others said I had this look of serenity about me, always calm and quiet, like a perfect picture. The name stuck—even if it didn't make much sense to the outside world."

"But it makes perfect sense when you're talking in code, right?"

"Right."

"You know what I wish?" she asked, hoping he'd understand. "I wish you and I could have a real conversation, no codes, no deciphering, or trying to twist or interpret Bible passages, just a real conversation."

She saw the blank wall falling across his face like a shutter slapping against a window. "Lydia, I know this is hard on you. You're away from everything you know and love. But—"

"But when this is all over, things will go back to normal for us? I don't think so. I'm not sure I'll ever be normal again." She touched one of the cool black joystick steering wheels in front of her. "I mean, I'm sitting in a Cessna, about to take off for parts unknown. I've gone from my first MARTA ride to my first private plane ride. Not to mention my first masked black-tie party, my first and only pair of stilettos, and my first ride on a watermelon truck. Oh, and I left out being shot at, being poisoned and almost being smothered. I don't think there is such a thing as normal anymore."

"Okay, I get it." He went back to his work, a frown furrowing his forehead. "Look, I have to get this plane in the air before they change their minds and call in reinforcements. Just be aware that they'll put a tail on us. People will be watching, waiting. It could get dicey."

"And what's it been up until now, a picnic?"

He let out a long sigh. "I'm sorry. I don't know what else to say."

She hated the way his broad shoulders slumped in defeat while his eyes filled with regret. Feeling contrite, Lydia dropped her hands in her lap. "No, I'm the one who should be sorry. I'm not usually so sarcastic and catty."

She looked out the cockpit window, staring out

into the night. The stars twinkled like a box of jewels set against velvet. Lydia felt as if she'd aged a hundred years in a few short days. But this wasn't over yet. She'd agreed to do this. She'd agreed to get in a plane with Pastor Devon Malone, in spite of all those superior warnings they'd been given back at Eagle Rock.

"I said I trusted you," she told him, her hand reaching out to touch his arm. "I meant it."

"I know," he replied, his gaze straight ahead. "And I appreciate you. So much."

He *appreciated* her. Not a mention of love or hope or kisses. He appreciated her. Well, wasn't that so very special. Lydia bit back the impulse to retort in kind. Instead, she said, "Well, I'm trying to work with you. I'm trying very hard to follow the commands and go with the flow. I'm sorry I got all snappy."

"You have every reason to be snappy," he said, lifting his gaze to her, his eyes holding hers with a blue as bright and flashing as the instrument panel. "Every reason in the world."

Lydia remembered Kissie's words to her, about how Pastor Dev would need someone there with him when all of this was over.

I'll be there, Lord, she silently promised. No matter the outcome. "I'll try to be more appreciative myself," she told Pastor Dev, her words quiet and level now.

"Okay."

He went in complete shutdown mode, just as he'd

done the night after she'd held him while he cried there in the roadside park. The man sure didn't like emotional encounters. He concentrated on getting the plane going, his every action precise and determined. And noncommunicative. Lydia felt so alone, sitting there by his side in the plane, the lights from the control panel illuminating them as they started off into the summer night.

She thought about her parents back home. She could picture her dad puttering around in his vegetable garden, gathering fresh cucumbers and tomatoes for all the neighbors. She could see her mother standing at the stove, frying up chicken for Sunday dinner, stirring the fresh cream peas she would have picked and shelled herself. There would be biscuits in the oven, sweet tea sweating in the refrigerator and a pound cake with fresh peaches waiting on the buffet in the dining room. Her whole family would be there right after church.

Did they miss her and wonder what in the world had happened to her? Lydia pushed the bittersweet images out of her mind, her prayers as silent and glowing as this still night. *I want to go home, Lord. I just want to go home. But before that can happen, I need You to help me. I have to be strong. I have to get through this with Your help. And I have to remember that Pastor Dev is a good man.*

Stubborn, hardheaded, determined, noble, fearless and downright aggravating. But he was still a good man.

Telling herself all these things, her prayers echoing over and over in her mind, Lydia took a deep breath and waited, bracing herself for whatever might happen next.

After Pastor Dev had been officially cleared for takeoff—they were on the Eagle Rock private airstrip and so they got whatever they needed, per CHAIM of course—he sat silently watching the monitors, his hands resting on the twin control sticks in front of him.

The screens displayed weather conditions, upcoming terrain and just about anything else they wanted to see. Lydia couldn't decipher much, but she saw what looked like a map on one of the screens.

"Where are we going?" she finally asked after her stomach had settled down. She hated flying, and being this up close and personal during a flight had left her a bit shaky and disoriented. But then, she reasoned, she ought to be used to getting shaky and disoriented by now.

He didn't speak for a minute, then he said, "I'm only telling you this because I don't want you to be surprised or alarmed. We're going to Colorado."

"Colorado?" She was certainly surprised and alarmed anyway. "Why?"

"Because The Disciple has a cabin there. And I think he wants me to come there. At least, that's the impression I got from his cryptic message."

"And what if he doesn't show up? What if—"

"He'll show. If he's truly in trouble and trying to find a way out, he'll know to come there. It's his secret place. Not many know about it, so he'll head there first. Either that, or he'll at least know we're safe."

"How can you be sure? I mean, what if it's another setup?"

She saw the flash of irritation in his eyes. "I *can't* be sure, so I'm going on instinct. I know Eli. I know how he operates. He wouldn't have risked everything by sending me that message if he didn't feel it was absolutely necessary."

"Okay, then. I guess I finally get to meet this notorious Disciple person."

"I think so. Either way, you'll be safe in Colorado."

"Famous last words," she retorted. Then she added on what she hoped was a more positive note, "I've always wanted to see the Continental Divide."

Dev hoped he'd managed to throw them off the trail. It hadn't been easy. After making a nocturnal stop on an "unofficial" airfield to refuel halfway through the flight, he'd been able to get them to Colorado and find the secluded landing strip that Eli had shown him years ago. And somehow, he'd handled landing the expensive plane in the deep valley between two jutting mountain ranges. That was a relief.

Now, convincing Lydia that they had to trek up the side of a remote mountain would be the next challenge. But if everything went according to plan, this would be their last trek, their last stop on this long journey to find the truth.

The truth. Dev let out a sigh, then started shutting down the plane. He had to wonder what the truth really was. For most of his adult life, he'd followed the dictates of CHAIM, because he had believed in everything the top secret organization represented, everything it had taught him—Christianity, amnesty, intervention and ministry. But now, he had to wonder if all of that was just a cover-up for a much more glaring and dangerous operation. What if someone high up in CHAIM had forgotten that mission statement? What if someone with unlimited power had taken that power and used it to his or her own advantage, without regard for the safety of Christians or God's word?

That would explain Eli's defection. That would explain Dev's gut feeling that something wasn't quite right. And that certainly would explain why someone was trying to kill him. Someone wanted his team to stay quiet. Starting with him. And maybe ending with Eli.

Because there was one glaring fact, one truth that Dev knew with all of his heart. If Eli Trudeau wanted him dead, Eli would have killed him by now. Eli wouldn't send others to do the job.

"We're here," Lydia said on a rush of breath, bringing Dev out of his thoughts. "I can't believe it. We're back on solid ground. I just might kiss the dirt."

Wishing he could take away her worries, Dev said, "Did my landing scare you that much?"

"Oh, not that much," she said, her tone light in spite of her wide-eyed expression. "Not any more than those fancy dips you did, or the fact that we traveled at nearly warp speed or how we had to constantly check for fighter jets scrambling to escort us to the nearest federal facility. I'm getting accustomed to flying beneath the radar, so to speak." Then she took another breath. "I just kept telling myself that God is my copilot."

He smiled at that. "At least you're still sure of the One in charge."

"Aren't you?" she asked, genuine concern etching her expression.

Lydia would fight all the hounds of darkness if she thought Dev was having doubts about his faith. That was one of the things he loved about her. He was beginning to think he loved a lot of things about her, but he had to block that realization out of his mind for now.

"I know God is in charge," he said to reassure her. "But right now, I don't know who in CHAIM is in charge. Someone is certainly trying to play God."

"Or someone is giving a very good impression of being one of the sons of God," she replied.

Dev felt a shiver of awareness go down his spine, an elusive memory just within his reach. "Say that again."

She frowned. "You know—the Beatitudes— 'Blessed are the peacemakers, for they shall be called the sons of God.'"

Dev felt the shiver turn into full-blown comprehension. He hit the steering control with such force, Lydia jumped.

"What's wrong?" she asked, grabbing his fisted hand.

"I think I just figured out who's behind all of this." He turned to face her. "Remember back in New Orleans when we met The Peacemaker?"

She nodded, then gasped. "I quoted that passage to him, didn't I?"

"You do remember," he replied. "You were kind of out of it, but you remember?"

"I remember a lot about that night," she retorted, her eyes holding his.

Putting their first kiss out of his mind, Dev nodded. "I do, too, but…Lydia, I think you summed this entire situation up when you quoted that passage to The Peacemaker."

She put a hand to her mouth. "You don't mean that kind old man is the one—"

"Eli told me to beware of the gray-haired man," Dev said, knowing he could trust her with this information. "I didn't tell the others because—"

"Because they were all gray-haired, more or less," she interrupted. "But the Peacemaker—" Lydia's eyes got even wider "—he was definitely gray-haired. And so helpful. Why would he help us if he's the one trying to kill us?"

"I'm not sure," Dev said. "It could be that he felt the heat and decided to steer us away—so no one would connect him to trying to do us in. It might be that Kissie's call alerted him—he had to play the part of friend and protector to hide his real motives."

"Why did Kissie call him instead of you?" Lydia asked.

"That's the question. She would have tried my

phone first. She knows to do that, but The Peacemaker implied she was afraid my phone wasn't clear."

"Are we sure Kissie is all right?"

"Last time I dared try, she didn't answer her phone, which is not like her at all."

"Try again," Lydia said, shaking his arm. "I don't want anything to happen to Kissie."

"Good idea." He unbuckled his seat belt. "Let's get out of this plane. It's got a big target on its back. And unfortunately, I left my Ruger back in New Orleans."

"I don't like guns," Lydia said. "And I especially don't like having a target on my back."

He hopped down, his mind racing as he ran around to help Lydia. Taking her into his arms, he became very aware of her clean fresh scent, of the way her hair fell in soft layers around her shoulders. She was still dressed in her cute capri pants and floral blouse, but she had been practical enough to exchange the flat sandals for a good pair of walking shoes, at least.

Because they'd be doing a lot of walking.

Lydia took his mind off both her prettiness and the road ahead. "Call Kissie."

Dev guided them away from the plane, to a clump of bushes near the deserted strip, then pulled out his Treo. "I've got a weak signal, but I'll try." She answered on the third ring.

"Valarie, how ya doing, baby girl?"

Dev frowned into the phone. "It's me, Kissie. Are you all right?"

"I am, but we have a bad connection."

"Is someone there with you?"

"You could say that, yes. The house is rocking tonight."

"Just tell me if you're safe."

"For now, yes. We could do lunch soon maybe. We have a lot to catch up on. I want to hear all about your vacation down south."

"South America?" Dev asked, his eyes connecting with Lydia's questioning gaze.

"That's right. Sand and sun, tropical flora and fauna. The works. I want to hear everything about that nice cruise. But, honey, right now, I have to go."

"I got you," Dev said, dread coloring his words. Kissie was trying to give him the rest of the story. "Stay safe," he said. "I'll be in touch."

"Right, Valarie," Kissie said into the phone, her tone light. "Remember trouble and anguish make us afraid—"

The line went dead.

"Kissie?" Dev stared at his phone, then looked at Lydia. "I think she's in trouble. She was trying to warn us about something."

"What?" Lydia came close, her hands on his arm. "What did she say?"

She called me Valarie. That's her daughter. Valarie. Why would she call me Valarie?"

"Maybe it was a clue," Lydia said. "Where does Valarie live?"

"In Florida." He thought back over the conversation. "She wanted me to figure out South America, so that means this *is* tied to that, just as I suspected."

"What else?"

"A cruise. She mentioned a cruise."

"Valarie, Florida and a cruise in South America," Lydia said. "They must all add up."

Dev closed his eyes and thought back. So much had happened down there and he'd tried to block most of it. "It's been a while. We were in a place called Rio Branco. It's the capital village of Acre, deep in the jungles of Brazil. It's a university town full of college students. We went down there to rescue a young woman from a religious cult that uses hallucinogenic vines to induce visions. Her wealthy parents wanted her home. We hired a boat guide, a trader, to take us up the river to a large *fazendeiros*—an estate, very large and lavish—that has to be what Kissie is talking about. The girl was being held on that estate. We never did find out who owned the plantation house."

He stopped, wondering how much more he should tell Lydia. "That's when everything went bad. She's confirming what I'd already figured out." But who was there with Kissie?

Lydia held his arm, steadying him. "Does this bad stuff have to do with The Disciple getting into trouble?"

"Yes." Dev looked up at the night sky and the mountains all around them. Telling Lydia this final truth would be just like climbing a mountain. "Let's get out of here and then I'll explain everything to you."

She let go of his arm. "Maybe she just called you Valarie off the top of her head. And Florida is tropical, like the jungle. She was grasping at ways to communicate."

"Yes, but the boat ride firms things up in my mind." He tugged her back toward the plane. "Let's get our backpacks," he said. "We'll need our supplies. We can talk on the way."

"Where is this cabin?" she asked as she slung the pack he handed her over her shoulder.

"Up there," Dev said, pointing.

In the newborn peaches-and-cream dawn, Lydia squinted up at the mountain face in front of them, then back to him. "You're kidding, right?"

"Afraid not," Dev told her. "We have to climb that piece of rock to get to the cabin."

Lydia looked back up at the craggy rock dotted with evergreens and shrubs as far as the eye could see. "This had better be worth it."

He took her by the hand. "We can go over everything we've put together, to take your mind off hiking."

She gave him a mock smile. "You are so very clever, but that's not funny." Then she squinted toward the east. "But that is certainly a beautiful sunrise."

Dev's phone rang, echoing eerily out over the trees and rocks.

"Hello?" His heart started pumping a hard beat. "Kissie? Are you clear?"

"As clear as can be expected, considering I just

had a nice visit with The Disciple. He was here, Devon. And he's very upset."

"What did he say?"

"Pretty much that he'd been set up. That what happened in South America was not your fault. He's not trying to kill you, Pastoral. He's trying to save you."

"Why me?" Dev asked, glancing around. They were exposed out here. And the woods could be full of secret watchers.

"Because…when you reported him as being too shaky to continue the operation down there, you apparently ruffled some big feathers. Whoever is in on this thinks you know something you shouldn't know. And they think you'll blow the whistle on the whole enchilada."

"But I don't have any information. I only know that after I told the truth, Eli lost everything dear to him."

"They did that as a revenge tactic, because he was too close to the truth and your trying to help him only confirmed their suspicions. Apparently, they're after him, too. And they think he told you something. Something that could ruin CHAIM for good."

"I don't understand—Kissie, it's been years and I don't know anything. Why now?" He stared over at Lydia. She was still and questioning. "I have to get Lydia somewhere safe. We're sitting ducks out here in the open."

"I have more," Kissie replied. "Eli said to stay at the hideaway until he can find you. His exact words to me were 'Tell The Pastoral to lie low.'"

"I plan on doing just that, but I need to talk to Eli."

"He doesn't want to be found, but he thinks they'll come there looking for him and you. He said he'd catch up with you very soon."

"Why didn't he just tell me this himself? Why didn't you put him on the phone earlier?"

"He wasn't the one with me earlier," Kissie said, her voice low. "I was stalling so Eli could get away."

"Someone else was there with you?"

"Yes."

"The Peacemaker?"

"He didn't identify himself. Tall, gray-haired. Implied he was my superior. But I'm pretty sure he's the man Eli told me to call the night of the Garden District party."

Dev let out a breath. "Eli called you and told you to call someone else instead of warning me?"

"Yes. He was rushed, but he made me promise to call a certain number. He said your life depended on it. I didn't ask questions. I called the number and got this man. Very cultured Southern voice. Very polite. He said he'd help."

"That's him," Dev confirmed. "The Peacemaker."

"I don't even want to know the rest," Kissie said. "Just get to wherever you think you should be. I've got to go. Things are very tense down here."

"Okay. Thanks. I'll figure something out."

"Oh, one more thing," Kissie said on a rush of breath. "The Disciple said to tell you—he has something you might want."

"What is that?" Dev asked, his whole being alert

to the sounds of the morning. It was a quiet dawn. Still and uncertain, like a rattlesnake about to spring.

"He has Lydia's diary," Kissie said. "And he's reading it page by page. It's very detailed, from what he implied."

"Lydia has a diary?" Dev looked at Lydia and saw her go pale. *A diary?* "You have a diary?"

She bobbed her head. "I keep a journal, yes. I left it at Kissie's."

"I gotta go," Kissie said. Then the call ended.

Dev stared at his phone, then let out a frustrated sigh as he looked sideways at Lydia. "What exactly was in your diary, Lydia?"

She shrugged, ran a hand through her hair. "A lot of things." She blushed. "Personal stuff." She waved her hands in the air. "I might have mentioned a few other things. You know, about us being on the run from the VEPs and…things like that. Right up until we left for the fancy party." Then she lowered her head and whispered, "Is that bad? Did I do something wrong?"

Dev didn't have the heart to voice the angry thoughts coursing through his head. "No, sweetheart, you didn't do anything wrong."

"Except put us in even more danger, right?" she asked, tears beginning to form in her eyes.

"Except that," Dev answered, his dread now at full throttle. "But hey, you keeping detailed records of our *every move* is just a minor point in the overall scheme of things."

He shouldn't have raised his voice. But he was

tired and angry. And, too late, he could see that same fatigue and anger in the misty reflection from Lydia's amber-flecked eyes.

Just before she threw her backpack down and took off in the other direction.

TWELVE

"Lydia, come back here."

"No." She kept walking, stomping toward the mountain. "Why don't you just go on and finish the job. I'll find a way out of here by myself."

"That's impossible. You'd never survive."

And he'd die before he allowed that to happen.

She lifted an arm in the air, waving him away. "That's just it. Poor little Lydia. So helpless and such a problem for everyone involved in this sordid operation. And apparently, I'm too stupid to live since I just happen to write in a journal—because, mercy, I wouldn't want to burden you with all my problems. I understand. I get it. I don't need to be here, and you don't need to be worried about me. So just let me go."

He looked down at the barren ground. "I can't do that. You know I can't do that. Lydia, I'm sorry. I didn't mean to imply—"

She turned then, her fury and pain piercing him like a golden lance as her eyes met his. "You didn't mean to imply that I've really messed up, but I saw it there in your eyes. I saw everything. And I understand everything. Your having to babysit me. If I wasn't in the way, you could do your job and get it over with. You could keep your secrets and your regrets close, without anyone else being the wiser, right? But I'm here and I left my diary in New Orleans because I couldn't bring it to that fancy party anyway, and then I was poisoned and we had to get out of there quick and now we don't know who's read it. I've put us in even more danger."

She brought her arms up, wrapping them around herself at midwaist, as if that action would protect her from all she'd seen and done. "I just want this to be over. Just tell me—when will this be over?"

Dev stood there, a few feet separating them, his heart going from hard and uncompromising to soft and yielding. He could yield everything for this woman. He would walk through fire to save her, to get to her. But right now, there was a big gap between his feelings and his duty.

"I honestly don't know how to answer that," he said. Then he couldn't stop looking at her, his heart warring with his head. "Lydia, please don't walk away from me. It's not safe. It's…"

He gave up with words. Instead he stomped toward her, and from the startled expression registering in her misty eyes, he must have looked like Sherman marching into Georgia. She didn't move, but he could tell she was holding her breath. When he got within inches, he grabbed her with one hand sliding around her waist. Then he pulled her close and put his arms around her.

Closing his eyes, he held her there, the scent of her floral shampoo washing over him like a cleansing breeze. "Lydia," he said on a whispered plea, "don't you know what you mean to me?"

She raised her head, drawing back to stare up at him, her eyes as shimmering and bronze as the sunrise glinting off the mountains. "No, I don't. Why don't you tell me?"

That simple request hit Dev square in the face, the dare in her words heating him with guilt and remorse. He couldn't tell her anything about his feelings. Not yet. Not now.

So instead of sparring with words, he went into action. He pushed his hands through her hair and kissed her. Not to calm her, not to stall her, not even to convince her.

He kissed her because he wanted to kiss her. And…he realized he wanted her by his side, not just to protect her and get her safely back home. But always and forever.

But first, he had to keep her alive.

Lydia felt so alive, so aware, so alert. They were standing in a deep valley between two twin mountains, and the man she loved with all of her heart was kissing her. As their lips touched, she realized two things. Pastor Dev cared about her, and he also had a job to do. He wanted to keep her safe, but not just out of duty. Now, now, there was so much more at stake between them.

Now, there was a chance for that always and forever she'd dreamed about.

If she'd just behave long enough to let him do what he had to do. He had every right to be mad about the diary. And she shouldn't have gotten so bent out of shape.

She drew back, a blush heating her skin. "I'm sorry," she said. "I should have told you about my diary."

He leaned his forehead against hers, his hands still caught in her hair. He stayed there a moment, then said, "It's okay. Even if Eli is enjoying all your private thoughts, he won't pass that information on to anyone else. And by telling us he has the diary, he's also telling us we can trust him. As long as he has it, no one else will ever get their hands on it."

Her blush went deeper. "I'd rather he *didn't* have it. It *is* very personal. And technically, it's a journal. A diary makes me sound like a high schooler."

He smiled at that, his words low and husky. "Did you write anything about me in there?"

Lydia was sweating now. She could feel a little trickle of dampness moving between her shoulder blades. "I'd rather not say."

The look he gave her made her fidgety. His eyes were a soft, sweet blue, as wide-open and all encompassing as the sky. "You did, didn't you?"

Wincing, she thought about the intimate passages of glowing, detailed adulation and love she'd professed there in her private ramblings. She might as well be an adolescent girl. It probably sounded that way. "Just a little. Will that compromise this mission?"

He laughed then, some of the tension leaving his face. "You're beginning to sound like an operative, sweetheart."

Like a real pro, Lydia tried to distract him from wanting to know more about her diary...uh, journal. "What can be done, about the situation?"

"Very smooth." He took her by the hand. "Let's concentrate on one worry at a time. Right now, we need to get up this mountain."

"What about The Disciple?"

"Kissie says he'll find us here later. Eli will come whenever Eli is ready. He'll want to make sure he's not being tailed. And he'll want to have all his facts straight."

"So who do we trust, The Disciple or The Peacemaker? Or should we be wary of both of them, and everybody else, too?"

"Good question, and probably a good observation—trust no one." He tugged her along over the rocks and shrubs. "Right now, however, I'm liking The Peacemaker for being the troublemaker."

"That nice old man gets a new name."

"Yeah, know any good scripture quotes for that one?"

"You reap what you sow," she shot back.

"You do know your Bible."

She was working on a retort when the first shot rang out.

* * *

"Get down!"

Dev didn't wait for Lydia to do his bidding. Instead, he pushed her behind an outcropping of rocks, their bodies crushing the delicate lavender columbines blooming nearby.

Holding her down, he scanned the distant trees and formations. When another shot rang out, he ducked down again, this time behind a sturdy shrub oak.

"It's coming from that copse of trees over there just beyond that ridge." He pointed to a spot about one hundred yards away from the plane where an outcropping of junipers and birch trees hung off the nearby hillside. "We need to get back to the plane."

"Why?" Lydia asked, her breath coming in huffs. "I mean, won't they see us?"

"Yes, but it's the fastest way out of here," he explained. "I'm not sure what they're shooting with, but if we head up the mountain, we'll be easy targets. And there might be more of them behind us, just waiting."

"Can't we just hide behind the rocks and trees?"

"They might have air support. They obviously tracked our flight." Which made him wonder if all the gray-haired men were in on this. He'd figured the CHAIM head honchos would put a tail on them, but he'd never figured they'd actually try to kill him.

Lydia grunted into the weeds. "Oh, right. Why didn't I think about air support!"

Glad she was back to her feisty self, Dev held her

down. "Listen to me, Lydia. We're going to follow these rocks until we can come around to the other side of the plane."

"Sure we are."

Another shot pierced the air. Dev held Lydia's head down. "They probably have rifles with scopes. It'll be easy for them to spot us. And there might be more than one shooter."

She huffed a breath. "Just like when we take the youth paintballing."

"I'm serious, Lydia. You have to stay down. We're going to crawl along the rock bed. Do you understand?"

"I'm not deaf or daft," she said, frustration coloring her words. "And I sure don't want to be shot. I've got it. Stay low and hurry up."

"And don't raise your head unless I give you the all clear."

"Got it. I'd like to keep my brain intact."

"Okay, then, you have to stay right behind me, so I can keep you out of the line of fire. Promise me you'll do that? And you have to stay low to the ground."

"I will. But…how are we going to get to the plane?"

"We'll figure that out once we get to the other side. I'm hoping the plane and that sun coming up over the mountains will shield us until we can get inside. And I'm praying whoever is up there isn't a very good shot."

"What if they shoot the plane down?"

"They'll try. But I'm going to get us out of here."

She didn't respond to that. Dev knew what she was thinking. *How in the world was he going to do that?*

Since he didn't have a clue, he could only act on instinct and years of training. "We'll be all right. Just follow me," he told Lydia, his breath winded. "Stay to my right."

She did as he asked, crawling along beside him. Dev dug his elbows into the dry rocks and sand, the grime of dirt, weeds and wildflowers sending up a cloud of dust. He glanced over at Lydia and saw her grimace each time they took a slow slide toward the next rock.

"I hope we have bandages in that plane," she hissed, the pain etched on her face causing her to draw in a long breath. "I'm going to be scraped to pieces."

"Just keep moving, sweetheart," he told her. "We're almost there."

Two more rapid-fire shots rang out, and this time Dev felt the whiz of a bullet as it passed right over their heads. "Lydia?"

"I'm here. That was so close, I think it split the hairs on my head."

"But it missed, right?"

"Yes. I'm right behind you."

They made it to where the plane sat at the end of the haphazard runway. Dev had tried to hide it near a group of aspen trees, just in case. Now that the "just in case" was here and they were being attacked, he turned to lie on his back, sweat and dirt merging on his face. "Okay, here's the tricky part."

Lydia let out a snort. "And here I thought we'd gotten past the tricky part."

He reached out a hand to her. She lay on her stomach staring over at him, then she glanced down at their joined hands. "I'm listening."

He saw the trust in her eyes and the little bits of columbine blossoms in her hair, and fell in love with her completely as they lay there in the dirt and flowers, with shots being fired all around them. Lydia never faltered, never gave up, even when she was fighting him tooth and nail. She might get weary, but she was still willing to fight the good fight. For God. And for him.

Because he saw the love in her eyes now, he could acknowledge that same love in his heart. Maybe it had been there all along, but now it shined brightly against the blue of the Colorado sky. So brightly, it almost blinded him with its hope and longing. He would not lose her now. He had to get her out of this mess.

"Are you ready?"

"As ready as I'll ever be. But, before we go—let's go over our list of options again."

He let out a sigh. "We don't have any options. If we go up that mountain, they'll track us and shoot us."

"We could just stay here until dark."

"And let them get in even closer? Not a good idea."

She glanced up toward the plane. "What's next then?"

"We're going to run to the plane, but you need to stay low to the ground. When we get there, squat down beside the back pilot's side wheelbase, okay? It's not much, but if you crouch there, you'll be shielded. Hopefully the rising sun and the thickness of those aspens will both work in our favor."

"Hopefully."

"I'm going to open the door on the pilot's side and I want you to get in as fast as you can."

"What about you?"

"I'll be right behind you." *Trying to keep from getting shot myself.*

"And then, you'll just crank her up and we'll take off?"

He didn't want to mention just yet that they didn't have much fuel. "Something like that."

"I hope that plane is bulletproof."

"If I know Alfred Anderson, it is."

He gave her hand a squeeze, then he leaned in to kiss her forehead. "Ready?"

"Absolutely." It was feeble and weak, but her eyes still held that look of trust and resolve. "Let's go."

Dev rolled over. It was too quiet out there, which could mean the shooters had given up, or that they were moving in. "On the count of three—" He ticked off the numbers, ticking off prayers inside his head while he said the words.

They rocketed out from behind the brush and shrubs, the sound of gunfire, closer now, rising to follow their paths. Dev prayed while he ran beside Lydia, his hand reaching to shield her and to try and keep her down as she moved. Bullets hit rocks behind them and bounced off the plane in front of them, but Dev kept pushing Lydia forward. "The wheel," he called to her. "Get behind that wheel."

Lydia dived toward the plane's tiny covered wheel, grabbing at the mushroom-shaped white metal covering, her body curling up in a tight little ball, her head down.

Dev scrambled toward the nose, then hopped around the plane to grab the door. Another shot rang out, then he heard Lydia's cry of pain.

And saw blood running down her arm.

Intense agony poured over Lydia as a scalding pain caused her arm to go numb. She looked down at the blood spilling against her hand, then glanced up in time to see Pastor Dev's hand snaking out toward her. She tried to reach him, but she felt sick, the waves of nausea rolling over her with the precision of a fast-moving waterfall. She was going to pass out.

"Lydia!"

She heard his voice coming through the roar of the blood pounding inside her temples.

"Lydia, take my hand."

The flare of more shots brought her head up. She blinked, lifted her good hand, now covered in blood, toward him. Then suddenly she was propelled through the air and into the cockpit of the plane.

Pastor Dev shoved her over the controls, causing her to cry out in pain.

"I'm sorry," he said on a winded breath. "I've got to get us moving."

"They finally got me," she said, her words weak and low, her eyes shut to the sight of blood. "Finally got me."

"You'll be okay," he said. "It's not that bad. Just a flesh wound. Thankfully, whoever's out there isn't a very good shot."

Or they'd both be dead right now. Lydia got that unspoken message loud and clear. Through the hum of pain rumbling inside her brain, she could hear the roar of the plane's engine coming to life.

Briefly, she felt his hand on her arm. "Try to put some pressure on the wound with your other hand, to stop the bleeding."

She grimaced, gritted her teeth and did as he said. "It hurts," she told him, her eyes tightly shut.

"I know it does, sweetheart, but you're going to be fine, Lydia. Do you hear me? I won't let anything happen to you."

"You don't sound convincing," she replied, thinking she liked him better when he was in his confident, commando mode. He sounded scared. She didn't like scared. But she knew he wasn't a coward. He was worried about her, scared for her sake. That brought a little bit of warmth and comfort to the pain coursing through her system.

She reluctantly opened her eyes, watching as he

turned the plane on a quick tailspin and got it lined up on the haphazard runway. The sound of bullets hitting the fuselage didn't help her mood.

"They're still shooting."

"I can see them now," Pastor Dev said, his hands moving over buttons and controls. "Two of them. They're on foot and they're lousy shots, so we have the advantage."

"What advantage would that be?" she asked, one eye open toward him.

He leaned back and looked straight ahead. "This."

The plane picked up speed and then in a matter of seconds, they were lifting off into the air, the roar inside Lydia's head now a steady match for the roar of the big engines. She felt sick all over again, but she swallowed back the queasiness and tried to pray her way back to being coherent.

Until she looked up and saw the mountain straight ahead of them.

"This isn't good," she said on a moan. "Not good at all. Do you see that big rock?"

"I see the mountain, but we're not going to hit it. It's farther away than it looks." Pastor Dev's gaze met hers. He started hitting buttons, his eyes going back to the screen. "And we don't have enough fuel to get very far."

"What?" Lydia sat up, dizziness clouding her vision. On the instrument panel, the lights were fading like fireflies, one by one. And the mountain which he'd just assured her was far away loomed straight ahead. Panic rising in her stomach, she tried to focus. Then she screamed, "What do we do now?"

Pastor Dev reached behind them, scrambling around until his hand hit what he'd been looking for. "We jump."

THIRTEEN

Lydia looked at the mountains around them, and then fixed her gaze on Pastor Dev. "Jump?" she shouted at him over the roar of the plane. "Did you say jump?"

He didn't answer. Instead, he hit some buttons and switches before climbing into the back of the plane, then turned and grasped her waist, lifting her up after him. He flipped her around and forced a harness over her head and down around her shoulders.

"This is gonna hurt," he said as he lifted her arms.

It did. She screamed out in pain as her wound throbbed a protest, then tried to push his hands away. "Let go of me."

"I can't," he said close to her ear, his hands working on shutting and snapping and arranging. "We have about a minute before we have to let go of this plane."

He was actually hooking them together, her harness connecting to the one he'd somehow managed to get around his own body. And she didn't dare look too long at the contraption attached to all of the harnesses and belts.

"Let go of the plane?" She shook her head, her gaze glued to the ever-approaching mountains all around them. "I don't want to let go of the plane. I want the plane to land again, with me inside."

She could hear him adjusting and fitting clunky things around them. He leaned in close, his voice coming in her left ear. "The plane is going to crash, Lydia. But we're going to bail out before that happens. It's the only way."

Lydia swallowed the fear and nausea roiling up from her insides like a giant tidal wave. "I can't do that."

"Yes, you can." He had his hands over hers now. "We're going to jump—it's called a tandem jump, actually more like a Mr. Bill jump. You'll be with me—hooked to me. All you have to do is wrap your arms and legs around me like a pretzel and hang on. I'll do the rest. But first, we have to get this door open and ourselves into the exit position. Piece of cake."

Lydia pushed his hands away. "You expect me to believe that?"

"I expect you to be brave and to stay quiet and to do exactly as I tell you." He dragged them both toward the exit door as he kept talking. "Don't worry, I've been trained in every kind of jump possible. I've got my jump wings, been through HALO and HAHO jumps. All part of the job."

His commando mode.

He was really going to throw them both out of this plane. Lydia prayed his HALO or HAHO or whatever it was he'd learned would be blessed. "I'm praying," she said, her breath heaving. "I'm just going to pray."

"That would be appreciated, sweetheart."

While he hooked and connected and checked and rechecked, Lydia looked at the mountains, looked around the plane, then squinted at him. "Is this our only option?"

"I'm afraid so," he said, kissing the top of her head. "And since this plane is going to tilt when we shift our weight, we have about twenty seconds to get ready."

Lydia let out a groan of fear and frustration. "I can't do this."

"You can do this," he told her, his voice calm and gentle and firm as he looked into her eyes. "We can do this, Lydia. Just look at me the whole time. I'll be right here."

She figured she had two choices on how she would die—in a plane that would surely crash into a mountain, or in the air as she plummeted to the rocky ground. She knew she wanted to go attached to the man she loved.

"Okay," she said, sniffing back tears. "Okay. But…Pastor Dev…promise me you'll hold on to me. Promise you won't let go."

"I won't let go," he said, his lips grazing her cheek, his head pressing against her temple. "I won't let go, Lydia. Ever."

She nodded, closed her eyes as she prayed for courage and strength. *No matter where I land, Dear God, please let us be together. I just want this to be over and I want to find peace in Your loving arms. And I want Pastor Dev to be right there with me.*

He started shifting them both toward the plane's door, explaining how they had to perch on the jump step, but Lydia refused to open her eyes. She kept praying, mixing the Lord's Prayer with the Twenty-third Psalm, just for good measure. "The Lord is my shepherd…I will fear no evil…thy will be done…on earth…forgive us our sins…the valley of the shadow of death…I will fear no evil…comfort me…the power, the glory…forever and ever…Amen."

Did God hear frantic, half-worded, sheer-out-of-terror prayers? She believed he was listening.

"Here we go," Pastor Dev shouted. "We're at around seven thousand feet in elevation. Time to go."

Lydia's heart seemed to stop beating then. Her whole body went rigid. She heard the door groaning, felt the tug as he helped her find a foothold. She felt the rush of a hard wind surrounding them, blasting on her skin, on her face. She couldn't, wouldn't open her eyes.

"Lydia, come on, sweetheart. We have to move close."

Somehow, she opened her eyes and did as he said, shifting her body along with his as they perched in the open door. "I can't—"

"You can. You have to. I won't let you die in this plane. I don't intend to let you die at all."

He explained their position and how he would free fall through the air. "I'll push us out," he told her. "We'll somersault and then…it'll be easy from there."

She nodded, her eyes shutting again. She couldn't breathe, couldn't speak. She just kept praying, her mind centered on her family and her world back home. Her safe, protected, sunny, wonderful world where fear and pain and evil didn't exist. She thought of the crape myrtles blooming along the streets of Dixon, thought of the giant magnolia tree in her parents' front yard, the ancient palm trees lining the city park. She could almost smell the gardenias blooming so bright white and sweet in her mother's garden. She could taste the sweet tea and the coconut cream pie her mother would have waiting for her when she got home. Then she thought of heaven and wondered if she'd be able to find Pastor Dev when they got there.

Heaven.

I won't be afraid, she told herself. *I refuse to be afraid. I can do all things through Christ, who strengthens me. I can. I can. I will. I will.*

"I love you," she said out loud, her eyes lifting open, her only thought that she had to tell him this before they both died.

He didn't answer. Instead, he looked straight into her eyes, then pushed them out into thin air. And all Lydia could feel after that was a strange weightlessness and a rush of pure adrenaline. Closing her eyes again, she felt the warmth of the sun, felt the brightness of the blue sky surrounding her, felt the warmth and strength of the man holding her and guiding her back down to earth.

She opened her eyes just as he pulled the rip cord.

And suddenly, they were floating, slowly and surely, as if they were dancers on a cloud.

Lydia felt his head over hers, felt the quick touch of his face to her hair. He managed a feathery soft kiss somewhere near her neck.

The rush of wind subsided as they neared the earth, and oh, my, what a view.

The mountains, some high and distant and still tinged with long-lasting spots of stubborn snow, sparkled in lavender and rose all around them, the rich greens of the aspen trees mingled with the lavenders, whites and yellows of the wildflowers covering the colorful valley beneath. A turquoise-colored lake came into view, bright and shimmering with waterfalls, its fresh blue waters making Lydia hold her head up as she breathed deeply.

"Is this heaven?" she said, relief and awe in her words as she gazed over at him. "Or are we still alive?"

"Not heaven yet, sweetheart," he replied, his eyes sparkling with hope and relief. "We're alive."

Then they heard it. The boom of the plane as it hit a far mountain and exploded.

The flare of the fire blinded Lydia, but the explosion was too far away now to hurt them. Floating here in Pastor Dev's arm, she felt as they were too far away for anything to hurt them. Ever again.

But she knew she'd have to come back down to earth very soon.

And then it would begin all over again.

She'd told him she loved him.

Had Dev imagined her words or had she really said that to him? Of course she'd said it. Lydia loved him. He knew that now.

He could have answered the truth, telling her that he loved her, too. More than he could have imagined, more than he had ever dreamed of loving a woman.

He loved her.

But unlike Lydia, he didn't have the guts to say that yet. Not yet. Not when he'd tried to hold back on his promises. Not when someone was determined to end both their lives. He had to make sure she was safe and back home in Dixon where she belonged. Only then would he feel that he had the right to tell her the same.

Right now, he had to land this chute and get her to a warm, safe place.

"Hold on," he told her as they came gliding down to the meadow. "Just lean into me and I'll catch us when we hit."

She did as he asked, and in the next few minutes Dev felt the thud of the earth meeting his body as the chute dropped and dragged them. Steadying himself, he gripped the suspension lines and tugged at the now-deflated chute as he fell toward the ground. His body took the brunt of the landing to protect Lydia.

"Let's get out of this thing," he said, hurrying to release the harness. After helping her out and up, he tugged free of the chute, then turned to her. "How you doing?"

"I've been better," she said, running a hand through her mussed hair. "No, strike that. I'm great. I'm fine. I'm alive." She grabbed him by the shoulders, tears shining thorough her smile. "We're alive."

"We are," he said, grinning down at her. "That was quite a ride."

"You can say that again. It was so…beautiful."

"Once you got past the thought of being hurled out of a plane, right?"

"Right." She stood staring up at him, her heart revealed in the rich coppers and soft greens of her shimmering eyes. "Right."

Then she turned to look around, but not before he saw the pain in those sweet eyes. She wanted to hear the words he couldn't voice.

"Where are we?" she asked, one hand grasping her hurt arm. She was covered in dirt and grime and blood, but she'd never looked more beautiful to Dev.

He wanted to pull her close and kiss her again. But that might only lead to a confession. He had a feeling if he held her again, he'd never want to let go. And he had to let go so they could get their lives back. So they could have a life together—without the shadow of danger hanging over their heads.

Pushing on, he tugged the chute up, working to pack it. They might need the material to make a tent later. "We're in Glenwood Canyon, somewhere just east of Hanging Lake. If I have my bearings, I-70 and the Colorado River are off to the west. But we need to head east."

She nodded, breathed deep. "It's so fresh and clean, so quiet."

"We could use some quiet," he said, taking her by the hand. "But first, I need to look at that arm."

He sat her down on a nearby rock, then held her arm out to inspect the wound. "Looks like the bleeding has eased up. How does it feel?"

"It hurts like all get-out," she admitted, wincing as he poked at the ugly gash just above her elbow. "But you were right. I think it just got grazed."

Dev thanked God for that. Things had happened so fast back there, he hadn't been sure if she'd been nicked or mortally wounded. He released a deep breath he hadn't even realized he'd been holding. All he could see in his memory was her face and the blood running down her arm. But she was going to be all right now. He'd make sure of that.

"We'll find some water and wash it out, at least. Then we'll cover it with some of the material from the chute."

She sat silently, letting him examine her. Then she halted his hand on her arm. Dev looked up to find her staring at him, her big eyes wide. "Where are we going now?"

He looked around, toward the east. "Well, I think I can find Eli's cabin. I remember once we hiked to Hanging Lake in a day and stayed to camp overnight, but it's been a while."

"And you think you can just take us straight there, through mountain and valleys and rivers and lakes?"

He nodded, smiled. "I do." Then he grinned. "I just took us through an almost impossible bailout, kiddo. You don't think I can accomplish getting us over another mountain?"

"I do believe you can," she said, returning his smile. "At least, I sure hope so." Then she quit smiling. "Will we be safe there?"

Dev prayed they would. "Well, since it's remote and extremely well-hidden and since Eli and I are about the only two people on earth who even know it exists, I'm banking on that."

"But…people are after us," she reminded him. "Those shooters—"

"Don't know that we survived the plane crash," he explained. "They probably think we're dead."

"Oh, and I guess that's to our advantage, right?"

He grinned at her businesslike words. "I would hope so, yes. At least it will give us some time."

"And what do we do when we get to this cabin? Just wait it out?"

That was a very good question. "I don't know, exactly. I have my Treo. If the battery works and if I can get a signal, we just might be able to do some behind-the-scenes work. But with the area being so far away from anything, I doubt that will happen. So we might just have to lie low for a few days, then hike out."

"Or we could pick wildflowers and frolic on the mountain."

He looked up at her then, and saw the hope in her eyes. "We could do that, yes. We deserve a little R & R."

"But…we'll be all alone."

Dev understood what she was saying, the reassurance she needed. "Yes, we will. But you're safe with me, Lydia. I would never do anything to compromise you…or embarrass you. You have to know that."

"Am I? Safe with you, I mean?"

The tight, clipped question took his breath away. "You don't think—"

She waved her good arm in the air. "I know you are a perfect gentleman. I know I can trust you. But what I'm asking, what I need to know and understand is…if my heart is safe with you."

"Your heart?" He hated to play dumb, but she was so direct and so beguiling and so cute and so hopeful, he had to stall just to find the right tactic.

"My heart," she replied, getting up to pace and stomp through the wildflowers. "You've rescued me, saved me, kissed me, pushed me out of a plane and done just about everything in your power to keep me safe and alive. But you have yet to sit me down and have a real heart-to-heart talk with me—about us, I mean. About what's happening between us."

He turned away. She pulled him back around. "Don't go all commando on me, either. Don't shut me out. I just need to know. I trust you with my life, but can I trust you with my heart? Because, I don't want to keep climbing mountains with you if I can't."

FOURTEEN

Here she was, traipsing up the mountain with him.

And he had yet to answer the burning question. The one about her heart.

Lydia huffed out a breath then turned to take in the spectacular vistas surrounding them. They were moving away from the stark orange-and-red canyon walls as they headed southeast. But there were plenty of hills and rocks ahead of them, literally and metaphorically. Lydia tried to concentrate on putting one foot in front of the other, instead of worrying about what was going on inside the head of the infuriating man beside her.

"You should know you can trust me," he'd said, just like that. "You have to know by now…."

Then he'd simply grabbed her and turned her toward the foothills. "Let's find some water."

Lydia had been so shocked, so flabbergasted, that she wondered now how her head had managed to stay on. She wanted to scream, really loud. But that wouldn't accomplish anything, except making her look childish and petty. Here she was, wanting a declaration of undying love from him, in the midst of running for their lives.

I am beyond help, she thought, her gaze tracing the lone flight of what looked like a hawk up above them. Wishing, for a moment, *she* could just fly away, she remembered their emergency parachute jump and decided she'd had enough of flying for a while.

"This way," he said, dragging her up a rock cluster.

Commando Dev. Intense, focused, confident, cool.

And scared to death of facing what his heart knew to be true. How could he not know? She'd told him she loved him. And she knew deep inside her own heart that he loved her back. She could see it in his eyes, in the way he protected her and watched over her. In the way he'd touched a kiss to her neck as they drifted to earth.

How am I supposed to convince him that his heart is safe with me, Lord?

Lydia didn't have the answers to that question. She'd just have to tough it out. But once this was over—

He stopped, causing her to lose her footing. Pastor Dev caught her against him, straightening her as he pointed ahead. "See that little stream just beyond the ridge?"

Lydia pushed her hands through her hair then took a calming breath. "Yes, I could use some of that water."

"We're headed there right now."

"Thanks for the update," she retorted, fuming with a smile on her face.

He kept straight on. "I want to get that wound washed."

"I want to get a bath."

"That might be hard to do. We need to keep moving."

"I was just wishing out loud."

He wouldn't look at her. He stared ahead as if his life depended on it, and Lydia reckoned it probably did. His love life anyway.

She didn't get it. This man was fearless in the face of mortal danger, deliberate and thorough in preaching the word of God, but he was a real wimp when it came to baring his own soul and telling her the truth. Didn't he know she'd take care of that part of things, that she'd nurture him, cherish him and love him enough to protect all of his carefully controlled defenses?

Apparently not.

"How much longer?" she asked, wondering if he'd get the hidden meaning of that question.

He didn't. "Not too far now. We'll stop and rest up at the stream, then one more ridge or two and I think we'll be near Eli's property. We should be somewhere between Four Mile Canyon and Dry Hollow. Eli's place is way off the beaten path, but I think we're on the right track."

"That's good." He was *so* off the right track for getting in touch with his emotions, she thought.

Maybe she should just tell him that, get him good and mad and talking. Talking in real words instead of tried-and-true clichés.

Off the beaten path. On the right track. "Whatever," she said, then realized she'd actually spoken that word out loud.

He finally chanced a look at her. Lydia hoped her smirk would get him riled, but it didn't. He just tugged her toward that welcoming body of cool water.

"Sit," he ordered, nodding toward a fallen tree on the water's edge.

Lydia sat, but not because he'd ordered her to do so. She was tired and thirsty and her arm was throbbing as if a woodpecker had chosen her arm instead of a tree. She pushed at her hair, wiped at the grime on her face then took another deep breath.

"Here." He pulled her around. "Can you reach the water for a drink?"

Lydia fell to her knees, then cupped her hands in the clean water, grabbing a handful of the glistening liquid to bring it to her dry lips. She took a long gulp, then another, letting the extra stream down her face. "That is so good."

Pastor Dev did the same, then washed his face and ran his wet hands over his hair. "Okay, let's get your arm cleaned."

Lydia didn't argue. She sat still as he gently splashed water over the deep gash. The water burned its way down into the ugly injury. "I'll have a scar," she said, looking up at him as the wound was washed clean.

He stopped, his fingers tracing the pink welt of the deep nick. He didn't speak. He just held his fingers there as if to heal her with the strength of his emotions.

And Lydia could feel the heat of those emotions, the warmth of his touch, pouring through her wound. She reached out a hand to his hair, pushing the short, damp strands back from his forehead. "It feels better."

He looked up at her then, his blue eyes blinding her with a need that mirrored her own, his words low and rough. "I think you'll have more than this one scar, Lydia."

He moved away from her to sink back in the grass and dirt, his wet hands moving over the five-o'clock shadow on his face. "How could I let this happen?"

Lydia felt a tug in her heart. Was he gearing up for some soul-searching? She sank back beside him. "It wasn't your fault."

He looked at her wound again. "Yes, it is my fault."

"You sure do seem bent on taking all the blame for everything. Why is that?"

He glanced away, out toward the mountains in the distance. A gentle breeze played around them, and he held his face up to the wind. "Because all of this is my fault, from the very beginning. Isn't it amazing, how one act can cause a whole ripple effect on so many people's lives?"

Lydia wanted to know what that one act had been. He'd hinted enough. Maybe he was ready to confess what he thought was his greatest sin.

"Are you going to hold it all inside? Or can you talk to me about it?"

He dropped his hands over his bent knees, shaking his head. "You know, I need to practice what I preach. I need to remember that I, too, sometimes need spiritual counseling."

Lydia glanced around. "Well, since I'm the only one available, you can talk to me. I'm not a trained counselor, but I am a good listener."

He looked into her eyes then, branding her with a sweet longing. "Yes, you are, that's for sure. You've always been my good listener. All those years we worked together, side by side—I can see it so clearly now. You were always the one I turned to, for advice, for guidance. You were my quiet strength, Lydia. My rock. I took you for granted, but no more. Never again." He shrugged, looked down at his hands. "But this…it's just so hard. I've held my secrets so close, for so long now—"

"We're in this together, Pastor Dev."

He touched a finger to the ugly tear in her arm. "Lydia, why don't you just call me Dev?"

Lydia should have been thrilled that she'd managed to jump over another hurdle, or in this case, get up another hill. But his request only made her want to cry. Her words trembled and tripped over her lips. "You'll always be Pastor Dev to me."

"No," he said, shaking his head. "No, things have changed. I'm no longer that man. And you've changed, too. It'll hit you once we get home. You'll be going along, everything fine, your life back to normal…and then, you'll remember the gunshots, or the reaction you had to the pesticides in New Orleans, or how you almost died several times over and you'll know that things will never be the same. You were right about normal, Lydia. There is no normal." He got up to stare down at her, his finger hitting his chest. "And I did that to you."

Not one to back off, Lydia lifted up toward him, grabbing him by the arms. "But you also did this to me."

She kissed him, her efforts gentle and sweet, her aim to show him that he hadn't ruined her innocence completely. He'd given her the strength to show him how much she wanted to love him. She kissed the lone tear that streaked down his face. She kissed the dirt smears on his jaw. She kissed the scrapes and scratches on his cheek and across his nose. Then she looked into his eyes, closed her own eyes and kissed him on the lips.

He resisted at first, but after a still, silent struggle she could feel with the intake of his breath, he finally gave in and returned her kiss. And for a brief moment, all the ugliness and bitterness was washed away, gone, forgotten. Forgiven.

Lydia pulled back to stare up at him, her hands cupping his face. "You did that, for me. You made me stronger. You made me follow my heart. And it brought me to you."

He backed away, gulped air. "Don't count on that."

Lydia felt tears piercing her eyes, but she held

them back. "Oh, but I am counting on that. I'm depending on you to do the right thing. Or rather to do the thing that you know is right—for both of us."

He turned to stare at the mountains, his hands on his hips. "We need to go."

Because she was bone-tired and highly alert to his denial, Lydia prepared to dig in her heels. "So you'll just turn away, shut down, refuse to let me help you the way you've helped me. Why is that…Dev?"

He pivoted to face her, his expression full of torment. "You don't need to know everything. I don't want to tell you everything. I'd like to keep part of you the way you were."

She didn't doubt that. He wanted to keep her as meek, mild-mannered, plain little Lydia. He wanted to keep her at arm's length, when they both knew she belonged in his arms. And he needed to be in her arms, too.

"Too late," she retorted. "Way too late."

That angered him. He stalked closer, his hand swinging through the air, slicing, chopping away at his frustrations. "You want to know and understand the real Devon Malone, Lydia? Well, here it is—the short version. I've betrayed my best friend to protect someone else I love. Eli was losing it down in South America. It had been a long, grueling mission, trying to find this girl who didn't want to be found and bring her home safely to her worried parents. Eli wanted to get home to his wife. She was eight months pregnant with their first child. I became concerned about him—he talked about getting things done his way. Eli always was a hothead, always impatient and hard to restrain, but he was so worried about his wife and child, he became careless. He was about to compromise the whole mission by just going in with guns blazing. So I discussed it with some of our superiors. They tried to take him off the mission, and he blamed me for that."

She held up a hand, shocked and confused, but determined to keep him talking. "What happened down there?"

"Too much happened," he shouted, his words echoing off the nearby mountains. "Too much. Before I brought things to a halt, Eli had been under-cover on his own, trying to get in with the powerful cult members. So instead of heeding my warnings and the orders from CHAIM to take a time-out, he went out on his own to keep things moving.

"We had to be so careful, we could only sit and wait. But Eli showed up again with the information we needed to go in and get the girl. We had to be very careful after that, and wait until we could find her. These people—they were part of a large drug cartel and they got suspicious. We think somebody tipped them off with the wrong information, because they thought we were undercover DEA.

"They followed us onto the river and ambushed the boat as we were bringing the girl out. The girl was killed. Eli and I got away, but he knew he was in trouble. And he blamed me for turning on him. He said some things—claimed I'd messed things up with my delays and worries. So now, he had our superiors on his case and these unscrupulous drug lords chasing him and threatening his family."

He stopped, leaned down, his hands on his knees as he sucked in a deep breath. "When Eli got home to Louisiana, his wife was gone."

Lydia gasped, her knees going weak. Sinking down on the fallen log, she looked across at him. "Dead?"

"Not at first. They took her, held her. We couldn't find her for a long time. Eli went berserk and disappeared, trying to find her, searching all over Louisiana and then down in South America. But…in the end, it was too late, we thought, for Eli and for his family." He stood then, tears streaming down his face. "We *thought* it was too late. We couldn't find Eli, but we finally found her. We tried to save her."

Lydia's heart was thumping so loud, she could hear it racing like distant thunder. "What do you mean?"

"His wife was in a coma for weeks. Weeks. But he didn't know. He never knew."

"You mean…you never told him?"

"We couldn't locate him. He was distraught and half-mad with grief. It was so bad that by the time CHAIM got to him…he had to be hospitalized. He was a threat to everyone, too dangerous and distraught to be out on his own. We had to get him some help, for his own sake. We sent him to a safe place to heal."

"The retreat?" she asked, swiping at her tears. "And that's why he blames you? Because you started this whole thing by trying to help him?"

Dev lifted his head. "In his mind, the time it took to delay the situation in South America, time used to control him and keep him from finishing the job, caused the problem. We could have been in and out, but I had to make sure he was up to it. So I held him back a few days, based on advice from CHAIM, and that gave this cartel time to get suspicious. Then we were compromised and we had to rush in after this girl and...everything just went crazy."

Lydia tried to state it in terms he could understand. "You failed at your mission."

"Yes, but worse, I failed my friend. I've failed him."

Which would stay with him a lot longer, gnawing at his soul, Lydia thought. "It wasn't your fault."

"Yes, it was. I could have waited until we were home, until we knew we were clear and safe. I could have made him take a rest, get some counseling. Retire maybe. I could have saved all of them, Lydia. Don't you see, I could have saved Eli and his family. All of them. But instead, I had to be self-righteous and sanctimonious, for the greater good. For the sake of CHAIM. I had to make a tough decision, and it was the wrong decision."

Lydia wanted to hold him, to help him. But she didn't dare touch him, not now when he was so caught up in his own misery. He'd only push her away again. "You did the best you could." Even that reassurance sounded lame and inadequate in the face of his pain.

He turned away again. "Well, my best wasn't good enough."

And suddenly, standing there in a wildflower meadow with the purple mountains' majesty all around them, Lydia understood why he couldn't tell her he loved her.

Because his best might not be good enough.

Because in his mind, he might fail. Again.

FIFTEEN

They found the cabin just before sundown.

Dev lay on a narrow ridge, his hand holding Lydia's, as he scoped the woods and trees. He had to be sure no one else had beaten them here. And without a weapon, he could only protect Lydia with his fists and his wits, both of which were not working at full capacity right now.

Protecting Lydia. That was his goal. But he was trying to protect her from so much more than the people who were after them, so much more.

He hadn't told her the end to the story.

And he probably never would. Too many people could get hurt, or worse.

"Let's take the back way in," he said now, pushing the dark thoughts out of his mind as he focused on staying alert. "I want to be sure no one else is here."

"We didn't invite anyone else," she said, back to her quick quips and wry retorts again.

Dev hated the way she'd gone all quiet and reflective after he'd bared his soul to her earlier. She'd stopped asking, stopped pushing, and now he had to wonder if she was so full of disgust and loathing for him, in spite of her reassurances, that she couldn't bear to hear any more details of his past. He couldn't blame her for that, not at all.

But, oh, how he wanted Lydia's respect again. And now he ached, wanting her love, too. She loved him; he knew that without a doubt. But love was a very fragile thing. It could quickly change to hate and resentment. He'd witnessed that with Eli. He couldn't bear that with Lydia. No, better to let her think the worst of him. Because whatever she was thinking now couldn't compare to how she'd feel if he told her the whole truth.

Determined not to let that happen, he guided her in a low crouch through the thick foliage around the perimeter of the square cabin, his eyes scanning the open pasture and winding stream that bordered the property. Then he glanced up toward the hills and ridges behind the cabin.

"A lot of hiding places around here," he whispered to her. "But maybe we won't get any company tonight. This place is so off the map, even CHAIM operatives shouldn't be able to find it."

"It's a beautiful place," Lydia replied. "Probably very peaceful and soothing in most cases."

But this wasn't like most cases, Dev reasoned. This was not a vacation. This was survival. "Eli always came here to find his center, to get his head together," he said. "I think he probably came here after South America."

Only Dev never had found Eli here when his wife lay in a coma, when she needed her husband by her side. Of course, Eli would have been on full alert back then. He'd probably left long before Dev even made it over the last ridge. Eli Trudeau had been raised in the swamps of Louisiana, so the man knew how to disappear.

He also knew how to reappear without warning.

And for all Dev could see, Eli could be out there right now, watching them, waiting to seek his own brand of vengeance. Dev would almost welcome that, if not for Lydia.

Taking her with him, he did a quick scan of the back of the house, where a tiny deck reached out toward the mountains. He didn't like entering a place cold, without benefit of equipment or weapons, but Lydia needed to rest and this was his last chance, his last hope.

Maybe Eli would come and they could get to the bottom of this once and for all or at least try to make things even.

"Okay, let's go inside and see how things are," he told Lydia. "Stay close."

"Like I'd run out into these mountains on my own," she retorted.

Dev didn't need to remind her that early this morning, she'd almost done that very thing. They both knew this had been the longest day—trekking through the mountains was hard work on a good day—but they were dragging a lot of excess emotional baggage. Or at least, Dev knew he was.

They crept quietly up onto the porch, then Dev kicked at the door, opening it wide. "No need for locks out here," he whispered. "At least never before."

He did a quick scan of the dim room, enough natural light left to allow him a clear view of the drab fixtures. It was a small kitchen. "No electricity," he whispered over his shoulder. "But I think I can remember where he keeps matches and flint. And there should be some oil lamps around here somewhere."

"What about food?" Lydia asked. "I'm so hungry."

"We might find some rations somewhere in here. There's an old well for water and washing, and he used to keep potable water on hand."

Dev held her behind him, protecting her with his body as they slowly entered the quiet, empty room. Then the hair on the back of his neck stood up.

Turning to Lydia, he put a finger to his mouth to silence any words. Pulling her close, he backed toward the door. What had it been? A sound, a soft creaking of wood? Maybe some nocturnal creatures scurrying away? But something wasn't right.

Something wasn't right.

At the door, he turned her around. "I think—"

"You thought right, bro."

Dev heard the familiar Cajun accent coming from deep inside the dark cabin. *Eli.*

"C'mon on back in, Pastoral. You're always welcome in my home, *mon ami.*"

Lydia gasped, stared at Dev with a questioning look.

Dev sent her a warning message to stay silent. "Eli, is that you?"

"Stupid question. This is my cabin, after all. Why wouldn't it be me?"

Dev held tightly to Lydia, willing her to stay quiet. "I thought you were going to take the long way back here."

Then they heard footsteps moving through the tiny cabin. And suddenly, Eli's body formed a dark silhouette in the middle of the kitchen.

"Hello, Pastoral. It's been a while." He bent his head, his expression full of caution and warning as he lifted his gaze toward Dev. "I tried to meander, you understand. Tried to get rid of the hound dogs on my trail, but—" He shrugged, winked, tilted his head to the left.

Dev tried to read Eli, careful to keep Lydia behind him. "But what? Are you ready to get things settled between us?"

Eli shrugged again, grinning, but Dev didn't miss the warning in his friend's coal-black eyes. "Me, I've got a lot of things that need settling." Then Eli cut his gaze away toward the left again.

That action brought another person into view.

Eli nodded toward the other man. "But him, he has even more at stake in this little game, *oui*."

Dev felt Lydia stiffen behind him, felt the fast-moving current of adrenaline flowing through his system as he stared at the man moving toward Eli.

"Hello, old boy. So good to see you again."

The Peacemaker was standing beside Eli. And he had a Colt .45 aimed at Eli's head.

Eli smiled, but the look in his dark eyes was deadly. "I told you it wasn't me, Pastoral."

Dev registered that, his gaze centered on the tall, gray-haired man holding Eli by the arm. "Why?"

The Peacemaker didn't respond at first. He just stood there staring at them. Then he said, "I don't have to explain my actions. I don't need to explain anything to you."

Dev glared at him, hating the smug, condescending expression on the man's face. His mind raced with ways to get Lydia out of this situation. He moved a fraction, holding her behind him.

"Don't do anything you'll regret, Pastoral," The Peacemaker said, his gaze slipping over Lydia. "She is such a pretty woman, isn't she? And so very hard to kill."

"You—" Dev rushed forward, and found the gun aimed at him.

Lydia screamed, moving forward, too. "What's going on?" she said. "I mean, why are you so determined to kill both of us? I don't know anything. I just want to go home."

Dev settled back, his arm pressed behind him to keep Lydia from rushing in with her own brand of justice.

The old man pushed Eli toward them, then turned the gun on all three of them. Eli sent Dev a look that said "How are you going to get us out of this one?" Dev wondered the same thing.

The Peacemaker shook his head, still glaring at Lydia. "But, my dear, you do know things. You now know all about CHAIM. Such a sanctimonious organization, don't you think? Taking the law into its own hands, so to speak. Seeking the ultimate justice where others have failed. You know our secrets now, dear, and you know my face. I can't allow that."

Dev noticed how Eli had moved closer, helping him to shield Lydia. A plan formed in his head. He knew he could count on Eli to get Lydia out of this cabin and keep her alive out there. He'd just have to distract this madman so they could make a run for it.

"Let her go," he told the other man, his hand slicing through the air. "She got caught up in this when you had my friend murdered in Atlanta."

"Didn't she, though?" The Peacemaker said. "And you, being so very noble, took her on the run with you."

"I had to protect her," Dev retorted. "I'm going to protect her." He sent a brief look toward Eli. "No matter what."

"Not if you're all dead," the older man said, his smile serene. "I had to abort my plan down in New Orleans, but I'm getting tired of chasing you all over the country." Then he nodded toward Eli. "But this one, he brought me right to you. Once I nabbed him, he was more than willing to help me out, just to save that crazy Kissie."

Dev looked toward Eli, giving him an expression of gratitude. Then he hoped his friend would see the signals in his eyes. *I need your help.*

Eli let out a snort, but nodded briefly at Dev. *Message received.* Then he made a big show, sighing, shifting, his expression serene and misleading as he cut his gaze toward The Peacemaker. "Now tell me again exactly why you need to eliminate all of us?"

The Peacemaker kept his gun trained on them. "It's a long story, really. Let's just say you both stirred up a hornet's nest down in Rio Branco. Your actions have jeopardized my operations there. You were trespassing on my estate, you see."

Eli grunted, then lifted his dark eyebrows. "You're a drug lord, *oui?*"

The older man laughed, held the gun higher. "That's such a derogatory way of describing it, don't you think? I provide a service to people. I have my own religion, my own way of teaching the word of God." He shrugged, shook the gun at them. "It's that simple."

"Why?" Dev asked again, needing to know how a supposedly good, faithful man could go so terribly wrong. But then, he reasoned, there was evil all over the place and some couldn't overcome the temptation.

The Peacemaker gave him a simmering smile. "It was just so…easy. The money, the power, the ability to control something. I had the perfect cover."

Dev nodded. "You used your CHAIM position and your connections. How could you do that?"

"Easy. I took what was offered."

Eli stopped smiling, and Dev recognized the deadly calm of his friend's whole countenance. "And you got rid of anyone standing in your way, right?"

"Unfortunate, but necessary. You two rushed in to save that silly girl, and, well, that brought too much attention to my little community."

Dev saw Eli's expression change, a darkness settling like a shadow on a mountain over his haggard features. "You killed my wife."

The Peacemaker didn't respond. He just stood there, a blank look on his face. Quiet came over the room as Dev watched Eli wrestling for control. Dev prayed Eli would stay centered and do what needed to be done to bring this man to justice.

"Did you kill my wife and my unborn child?" Eli asked, his fists clenched tightly at his side, his eyes as wild and dark as a forest creature's.

"I'm so sorry," The Peacemaker said, his voice filled with a false inflection of pain. "If Devon here hadn't reported your extracurricular activities, that might not have been necessary. But when he brought your noble mission to a halt and you went off snooping on your own…well, things just got too hot. I couldn't take that risk. I mean, how would it look if one of your CHAIM superiors was accused of being the head of such a mighty cartel? Not good at all. Especially considering that poor girl also knew too much about me. I couldn't let you rescue her and return her home. I'm very sorry, truly I am."

Dev felt sick inside, seeing the deranged gleam in the man's eyes. This man, so high up and such a legend within the ranks of CHAIM, had turned into an evildoer of the worst kind. Murder, drug trafficking, illegal activities, and all beneath the guise of helping Christians. Dev felt such shame washing over him. It was he who had brought them all to this moment.

Then he heard a voice as clearly as if someone were standing right beside him. "Not you. But him."

Dev felt a new courage pouring over him. He looked toward Eli, saw the rage and torment there in his friend's dark eyes. But he also saw something else. Eli's eyes shone with a new understanding, a new hope and a forgiveness that had not been there since the awful events of that day.

Dev knew what he had to do. He had to make this up to Eli and he had to save Lydia. He could almost read Eli's thoughts. *Now, bro.*

Stealing himself, Dev said a quick prayer. Then he stopped thinking and went on adrenaline and impulse. "You will not get away with this," he said, just before he lunged toward the man holding the gun.

The gun went off and the fight was on.

Lydia screamed, her mind going numb as Pastor Dev moved like lightning toward the other man. She heard the gunshot, saw the two men engaging in an all-out battle. But before she could see if Pastor Dev had been hit, she was dragged away.

By him. By Eli Trudeau.

"Let me go," she shouted, kicking and screaming as he lifted her up and stumbled out the back door. Lydia's efforts were fruitless. The man was solid muscle, as tightly built as an iron freight train.

"Let me go," she cried, glued to the open door,

tuned to the noises coming from within. She could hear crashes, shouts, grunts. "I have to get back to him."

A big hand came over her mouth as Eli set her on her feet behind a jagged rock. "Shut up," he said into her ear, his tone almost conversational. He wasn't even out of breath. "If you behave, I'll take my hand away. Don't make me have to gag that cute mouth of yours."

Lydia tried to reason that this man was on their side. Or so Pastor Dev wanted to believe. But what if this were a setup to get her away from Pastor Dev?

She decided in order to keep herself alive, she would pretend to be docile. For now. So she slumped down, nodding toward the man holding her as she slanted her head around.

"That's better." Eli pulled his hand away, then hissed in her ear. "Don't make a sound."

Lydia didn't dare breathe. She waited, listening for more gunshots. All she could hear now was her own unsteady breathing. And a long sigh from the man behind her.

"We're sure up the creek without a paddle, *chère,*" he said. "I need you to listen to me."

Lydia sure knew this drill, but she was so worried about Pastor Dev, she couldn't think straight. "But what about—"

"Devon knows how to take care of things in there," he retorted before she could even form the words. "He'll be okay."

"Not if he's wounded." She squirmed around to

face her captor. Then stood silent as she got her first good, long look at the notorious Eli Trudeau, aka The Disciple.

He was just a tad taller than Pastor Dev. He was dark, bronzed and baked like a golden statue. His hair was so dark, it shimmered almost black in the growing dusk. His eyes were the same way—dark, intense, brilliant with secrets. She was both intrigued and terrified.

"Hello," he said, glancing back toward the silence coming from the house. "I'm Eli."

"I know who you are."

"*Oui,* and I know who you are. Your journal was very detailed."

She wanted to smack him. "Where is my journal?"

"In a safe place."

Lydia didn't have time to dwell on that. "Are you just going to stand there, or are you going to help him?"

"I am helping him, by keeping you out of the fray."

She pushed away from him. "I can't do this. I can't let him die just so I can live."

"He would want it that way."

"I *don't* want it that way."

He shrugged, held a hand up to block her way. "I can't let you go back in there. I have to honor Dev's wishes."

"How do you know this is his wish? And how do I know you're not in on this? You could easily let him die, then kill me."

"I could do that, very easily," he answered with another eloquent shrug. "But not today, love. Not today. Today I have to keep you safe while Dev finishes up in there."

"So we're just going to stand here all night and let him do battle with that evil man?"

He shook his head, his long hair falling around his grizzly face. "*Non,* I didn't say that, now did I?"

Lydia saw the glint in his dark eyes. "I hope you're the man Pastor Dev says you are. I need you to prove that to me."

He grunted, pushed a hand through his hair. "I don't need to prove anything to anybody, but I do owe my friend in there."

"Which one?"

"You don't trust—that's a good thing."

"I don't trust. You're right on that."

"Well, then we have a little problem. Because I can't do my job if you don't behave."

"And what exactly is your job right now?"

"To get you as far away from this cabin as possible." He took her by the arm. "So c'mon."

"No." She pulled and tugged, but it was as if an iron vise had her arm in its grip. Then she tried pleading. "Please, don't leave him in there. He'll die."

"He won't die. But he will get us out of this. You have to count on that."

"I can't," Lydia said, tears spilling down her face as he shoved her up the mountain. "I can't leave him."

Eli didn't respond. She saw the unyielding gleam

in his eyes, though. This man wouldn't relent. So she'd just have to find a way to get back to Dev herself. And she'd just have to be the one to save them all.

SIXTEEN

He was alive.

That at least made Dev feel triumphant.

He was also tied up and in intense pain from the gunshot wound in his left leg. The bullet had passed through, but its path still throbbed and pulsed in protest. But that pain didn't bother him as much as the relief of knowing Lydia was still alive, too. For now.

In the muted light from a single kerosene lamp, the other fellow didn't look so good, either. The Peacemaker had fought valiantly, the force of evil propelling him with an almost superhuman strength. If Dev hadn't been wounded, he might have been able to take the older man. But he *was* wounded and that slight distraction had cost him his freedom.

And given Lydia hers.

He prayed Eli would know what needed to be done. He hoped Eli would get her to safety, then disappear for his own sake. But if Dev knew Eli, and he probably knew the man better than most, then Eli would be back here very soon to end this thing one way or another. Especially since Eli now knew this man was responsible for the death of his family.

But Dev wasn't going to sit idle while that scenario stewed. He had a plan. He always had a plan.

"You've worn me out," The Peacemaker said from his place across the floor. He was leaning in front of the empty, silent fireplace, winded and wounded, his gun at rest beside him. "I do believe you cracked a couple of my ribs."

"I'd like to do more," Dev countered, hatred and loathing filling his soul. "You've caused the people I care about a lot of pain. And all for drug money."

"Not to mention a nice estate in South America, cars, planes, boats and beautiful women."

"You don't have a conscience, do you?" Dev asked, amazed at how calm the other man seemed to be. "Don't you know you won't get away with this?"

The Peacemaker laughed, shook his head, streams of dirty sweat pouring down his face. "But I have, for years now. And once I eliminate you and those other two out there, my life will go back to being wonderful."

"You might get rid of me, but you will have to answer to a higher source for your sins."

The Peacemaker held up a hand. "Spare me, please. I don't need a sermon on my eternal soul."

"No, you don't need it, but you're sure going to get one when you go to meet your maker."

"I think I'll be just fine," The Peacemaker replied, his whole demeanor one of calm assurance. "All of this getting through the narrow gates stuff is rather silly, don't you think?"

Dev couldn't say what he was thinking, but it didn't have anything to do with the narrow gates. "When did you switch over to the dark side?"

He looked away at that. Dev watched him carefully, saw the change come over his demeanor. The Peacemaker went from being hostile and angry to quiet and reflective. "When I lost my son to CHAIM."

That brought Dev's head up. He was still a minister and a counselor, after all. "Want to talk about it?"

"I do not. Let's just say that I didn't appreciate how he gave his life for what is supposed to be such a fine, Christian organization."

"We all take that risk when we sign up," Dev pointed out, hoping to get to the heart of this matter.

"Do we? Or are we brainwashed and persuaded into doing someone else's bidding in the name of God?"

"Do you feel that way?"

He looked back at Dev then, his eyes feral in the yellow lamplight. "I didn't at first. But...you see, Pastoral, I was the one who convinced my only son to join up with our legions. He did something in his youth that I found scandalous, so I thought he might learn a valuable lesson from being amongst our ranks. I never dreamed he'd be killed at such a young age."

"So you're blaming yourself right along with blaming God?"

Anger unfolded like aged parchment paper over his wrinkled face. "I blame God for making me think we were all invincible. I blame God for taking my son. After he died, I died inside. I didn't care anymore." He gave Dev a long, hard stare. "There is nothing noble left in me, you see."

Which meant he had nothing to lose, Dev reasoned. He could almost sympathize with this tired old man. Except that this tired old man had killed people in order to appease his own torment and guilt. Why hadn't he turned to God, instead of away from Him?

Dev thought back over his own career in CHAIM, wondering to whom this man was referring. "Can you tell me his name? Your son, I mean?"

"He died years ago, before you were ever in the organization. You don't need to know that."

"I can find out on my own."

"Not if you're dead."

Trying to keep the man talking, Dev said, "If you want me dead, why didn't you kill me when you had a chance? Why did you wait for five years?"

The other man brought a knee up, then placed a hand across it. "I did think along those very lines myself at first. I almost came after both of you right after you left South America. But my operation had been compromised and it was too dangerous. I had to bide my time and stay the course in CHAIM. So I waited until The Disciple was released, then put my plan into action—killing you to set him up, thus eliminating him from CHAIM forever. But of course, that plan went awry in Atlanta. I became so angry after that failure, I wanted to see you suffer just as I had suffered. So I decided to eliminate the girl, then you. I thought by killing someone you care so deeply about, I'd have my revenge."

Dev didn't flinch, but that image gave him cause to push on. "Well, why didn't you do that?"

"You foiled that plan, over and over. In Atlanta, in New Orleans, even at that fortress at Eagle Rock. It became so very tedious, sending incompetent people to do the job."

"So you weren't in all of those places?"

"No, I sent underlings and new hires to do my work. They are always so willing to please, but they are also very inexperienced and stupid. When I realized things were going wrong in New Orleans, I directed you and the woman toward Eagle Rock, this delicious sense of justice in my mind. You know, kill the woman, distract the agent, all the while looking like the concerned superior I'm supposed to be, that sort of thing. Alexandre let me down on all accounts, however."

"Thank goodness," Dev said, meaning it. He couldn't think past what would have happened if Lydia had died there. He surely would have wound up like Eli—at some remote retreat trying to get over an unimaginable grief. Which is obviously what this man had wanted.

"I had to take matters into my own hands," The Peacemaker explained. "I had to track The Disciple down. I knew he'd lead me to you. He might be bitter, but his heart is still weak. I had to keep tabs on him and use him."

"Ah, because you'd so carefully set it up to make him look like the guilty one."

"A perfect solution. That man has always been a thorn in the side of CHAIM." He waved a hand in the air. "And now, here we are."

"So…get it over with," Dev goaded. "Kill me."

"I can't do that just yet, old boy. I have to wait for the girl to come back."

Dev's heart lurched at that remark, said in such a conversational voice. He didn't want to think about that scenario, and he couldn't let it distract him now. "She won't be coming back."

"Oh, but she most certainly will. She's in love with you. And we both know love is a very powerful tool in this business. Even The Disciple with all his muscle won't be able to hold her back." He laughed low in his throat. "That's the only reason I'm not out there tracking them down. I can rest here and know she will find a way to return to you. And that you, in turn, will die for her."

Dev sat staring at the other man, thinking no truer words had ever been spoken. He loved Lydia; he was willing to die to save her. This man, whoever he was, had loved his son, and he was willing to turn to evil in order to appease that love. A thin line…a very thin line.

And Dev could see that line drawn very clearly between his kind of love and the kind this man had tried to justify.

But sitting here, he also knew that God understood all motives and all suffering, and all forms of love, good and bad. So he prayed for Lydia and Eli and himself.

And he prayed for The Peacemaker, too.

She was praying.

It was full dark now. The Disciple had her up on a ridge, in a spot where he had a clear view of the cabin below. They were hidden here, but Lydia felt completely exposed.

Because he was watching her like a hawk.

She had to figure out a way to sneak past him and get back to that cabin. Maybe if she got him talking.

"You sure are a man of few words," she said, her voice calm in spite of her shaking hands.

"Not much to say at this point, *chère*."

"Tell me about yourself, your life."

"No."

"I'd like to understand you better."

"No one can understand me *better*. I'm beyond all understanding."

"Pastor Dev understands you. He tried to help you."

He went so still, she wondered if he'd turned into rock. "*Oui,* he certainly did. But he should have stayed out of it. He didn't know what he was getting involved in."

"You can't blame him for what happened. All of this is that man's fault. That man down there who's holding your best friend—he's the one to blame."

He whirled, fists clenched. "You talk too much."

Lydia glared up at him. "I want to go back and help Pastor Dev."

He got up, moved around the makeshift camp he'd erected. All in all, he wasn't a bad host. He'd found them water on the way up the mountain, and he'd offered her some sunflower seeds he'd managed to smuggle into the big pocket of his frayed cargo pants.

But Lydia could tell this man did not like sitting still. He moved around like a caged panther, ready to strike at any time. Lydia didn't know how she was going to get away from such a fierce warrior.

But she was going to, somehow.

She watched him pace, saw him glance back toward the cabin. Maybe he had a plan, too. While Lydia was waiting for him to reveal that plan, she found one of her own. There was a big branch from a fallen tree near her feet. She could yield that as a weapon. She wouldn't kill him; she'd just knock him down long enough to make a run for the hills and then on to the cabin.

And she'd be carrying that big stick with her when she got there.

Dev woke with a start. He hadn't meant to doze off, but his leg was throbbing with all the precision of a marching band, beating at his fatigue, dragging him down. He so wanted to sleep for a good week, at least. But he had to stay alert.

"Don't worry, old boy. I'm not going to fall over in a slump," The Peacemaker said, his gaze centered on Dev. "Unlike you, I can't sleep. I'm watching for the lovely Lydia. She'll be here soon. I can feel it. The night is so still. Not a breeze stirring. This canyon is waiting for something to happen."

Dev imagined Lydia was doing the same. And Eli, too, he hoped. He hoped Eli was making sure Lydia was far away from here and safe. And reinforcements would be coming soon.

But then, Dev couldn't be completely sure of Eli's motives, either. Surely he wouldn't hurt Lydia just to get back at Dev. But he had brought this man right to their door. Eli could have easily outsmarted The Peacemaker, so why hadn't he? Maybe he did it for Kissie's sake, or maybe that had been a convenient cover for his real motives.

An uneasy feeling settled over Dev then. He couldn't just sit here, waiting. He'd done enough waiting during this whole ordeal, thinking everyone else would help Lydia and him. That had only brought more trouble. He had to get away from The Peacemaker and find Lydia. He had to end this thing, one way or another, tonight.

Lydia bided her time. She could be very patient when she had to. She prayed, sometimes out loud.

"'Blessed are those who mourn, for they shall be comforted.'"

Eli whirled to stare down at her. "You are seriously getting on my last nerve."

"I have to stay calm. Praying and quoting scripture helps me to stay centered."

"Well, I have to think, so pray silently, okay?"

Lydia shook her head, managing to ease toward the big stick. "I thought the prayers might bring both of us some comfort."

He grunted. "I said to be quiet."

Lydia pretended she didn't hear that command. "'Blessed are the merciful, for they shall obtain mercy.'"

He kicked at a rock, then scoffed at her. "Mercy? Do you see any mercy around here, *catin?*" He bent close, wagging a finger in her face. "That old man down there shows no mercy. He is hard and mean and callous. He always was."

"You know him?" Lydia asked, slipping closer to the thick tree branch. Bending over, her hands on her knees, she managed to roll it underneath her sneakers. "How do you know The Peacemaker? I mean, you've been with him for a while now, obviously, trekking all the way to Colorado—"

"We flew here on his private jet. It was a quick trip. He did most of the talking."

Lydia could picture that. This man did not like to give up words. "Okay, then I guess you learned a few things about him then, right?"

Eli threw his hands up in frustration, then bent over her again. So very close. "I didn't have to get to know him. I've known him most of my life."

That admission sent up warning flares in Lydia's mind. If The Disciple already knew The Peacemaker, then they could indeed be in on this together. "Are you holding me here so he can kill Pastor Dev? Are you in this with him, just to get revenge for whatever you think happened in South America?"

He glared down at her, his silhouette dark and forbidding in the moonlight. "What are you saying?"

"I'm saying, I don't like the way you're handling this," she told him as she carefully rose to her feet. She had the limb in one hand now and hidden behind her back, the benefits of darkness and shadows working in her favor. It felt fairly solid, even if the weight was causing her hurt arm to protest. "I'm saying you're just stalling and I don't like that. I want to know why we're just sitting here, when we should be down there helping Pastor Dev."

"Because I know better than you how to deal with this situation. We wait until it's good and dark, then we make our move. But we're not going back to that cabin. I have to get you away from here. You know too much already and you don't need to see anything else. For your own good."

"Pastor Dev has been telling me the same thing for days now," she retorted, good and mad at the lot of them now. "I'm so tired of hearing that. I can think for myself and anyone can see that you're holding me here for your own purposes. Pastor Dev—"

He stood up straight like a bear rising, smiling then, his arms crossed over his barrel of a chest as he jeered at her. Arms still crossed, he leaned down again. "That's real cute, for true, the way you call him Pastor Dev. I read all about how you love him so much—there in your journal. Sappy stuff, that. Pastor Dev this, Pastor Dev that. Oh, Pastor Dev, I love you so much. Oh, Pastor Dev, I'm praying for you. Oh, Pastor Dev, I love your superhero T-shirt."

"You shouldn't have taken my journal. That's private."

Looking down at her, he shook his head. "You are so out of your league, *catin*. If I hadn't found that book at Kissie's, we'd probably all be dead now. You wrote about—what did you call them—the VEPs. You didn't name names, but you had evidence. Strong evidence, tracking both of you from Atlanta to New Orleans. You need to learn to keep your mouth shut and your pen dry. CHAIM does not operate in a tell-all fashion. So be glad I hid that journal for you."

"After you read it, of course."

"I read it to get clues—and I thank you for that, at least. But, *oui,* I could have done without all the mushy love letters."

Lydia's anger and shame caused her to find the strength she needed to bring the broken limb up. With a swiftness that had him lifting his eyebrows in surprise, she brought the heavy limb around and managed to land a sharp whack on his head, right above his left temple. Then she watched as he stumbled and fell down, his hands flailing in the air. He wasn't out completely, but he was rattled. He came to enough to hear her next words, though. And since she knew he'd be up and after her soon, she shouted as she was backing away at a fast sprint.

"I do love him. And that's why I'm going after him."

SEVENTEEN

Everything after that happened in a blur of darkness and shadows. Lydia ran down the mountain, keeping her eyes on the single light shining from the cabin below. Thank goodness she'd memorized landmarks and rock formations on the way up, or she might have been lost in the wilderness for a very long time. But she knew God was leading her; she wouldn't lose her way. So she stayed the course, all the while aware that Eli Trudeau was right on her heels.

She heard him call out. "Don't be foolish, Lydia. You're going to get all of us killed."

Lydia kept on running. If she died tonight, well, at least she could die knowing she tried to help the man she loved. She was stronger now than she'd been a week ago. Never again would she be meek and mild Lydia. Now she would be assertive, firm Lydia, sure in her faith and even surer in her path in life.

And right now, that path was leading straight to that little mountain cabin.

* * *

Dev waited for just the right moment. He was tired, thirsty, hungry and hurting, but a rush of pure adrenaline had him on high alert right now. Something didn't feel right. Something was about to happen.

He watched as The Peacemaker paced in front of him, his gun held in place to keep Dev still and cooperative. Dev wasn't afraid he'd be shot again. But he was deathly afraid that if he made a wrong move, Lydia would die.

He still hadn't put it all together, but his analytical mind had pretty much figured most of it out. The Peacemaker had been running drugs for years now, under the guise of working for CHAIM. And somehow, Eli must have found out more than he'd let on. Then in true Eli fashion, he'd gone off by himself to fix that wrong. But why had Eli almost gone off the deep end down there? Why? Dev just hoped Eli would come clean on that angle and finally end the mystery once and for all. Whatever the case, when Dev had brought things to a halt, someone had inadvertently alerted The Peacemaker and then everything had gone wrong.

Now they were after Dev, at first making it look as if Eli was the one seeking revenge. The Peacemaker had certainly been patient, waiting to strike exactly when Eli was released from his "retreat." But there was one missing piece to this entire puzzle. Why hadn't The Peacemaker killed Eli already, since Eli obviously had the goods on the man's illegal operations? Why had The Peacemaker let Eli live for five years, when he could have so easily had him murdered either at the retreat or now when they'd been chasing each other all over the country? And why hadn't Eli told anyone about what he'd found in South America? Why?

"You're very quiet," The Peacemaker said now, whirling to stare down at Dev. "Are you contemplating meeting your maker?"

Dev laughed, shifted his weight, grimaced as pain shot through his leg. "No, actually I'm contemplating how you managed all of this. I've pieced together most of this equation, but I have yet to understand the connection between you and Eli. There has to be one."

"Of course you'd figure that out," The Peacemaker replied, nodding. "That, my dear boy, is a rather long and sordid story."

Before he could get an answer to that burning question, a commotion from outside caused The Peacemaker to hurry to the back door, his gun at the ready as he slowly opened the door a few inches.

Which presented Dev with the opportunity he'd been waiting for. It was now or never.

Lydia cried out just as she reached the clearing leading to the cabin. She was once again being held by a set of supersized arms. Eli had caught up with her.

"Let me go," she hissed, tears of frustration falling down her face. "I have to help him. I have to—"

He held her, but his grip gentled as he leaned close, whispering into her ear. "I understand that, honey, but you need to understand something else. You can't do it alone."

Somehow, Lydia heard the sincerity and the resignation in his words. "Will you help me, then?"

She felt his nod. "*Oui,* although I keep thinking fools rush in—"

"Where angels fear to tread," she finished, gulping back a sob. "What are we going to do?"

"Well, you've foiled my attempts to keep you out of harm's way, and you made enough racket to wake up the whole mountain, so we don't have a choice except to go back in for a nice little visit. But I do have a plan. I always have a plan."

"Just like Pastor Dev," she said, tears falling from her face to land on his big hand on her arm. She could see the wetness glistening in the white wash of moonlight. "Thank you."

"Don't thank me until it's over."

"It will be over soon," she replied, her silent prayer echoing that sentiment. "So what's your plan?"

Eli pushed her away. "I'm going to surrender myself to The Peacemaker. He's really after me anyway, you see. We both know that, but he's been stalling, hoping to get in three kills with one strike, so to speak. I need you to stay right here and wait for Dev. He'll come for you soon, because I'm about to give him a head start. I'm going to be the first kill."

With that, he took off toward the cabin, calling out

in a loud voice, "Hey, old man. Go ahead on and get this over with. Take me out and let them go. The girl doesn't know anything. And Dev is a good man. Besides, I never told him anything about what I knew. And I never will. So let's end this thing now, just you and me. What do you say, *Grandpère?*"

Grandfather?

Lydia gasped as she rushed forward. At about the same time, the cabin door came crashing open as Pastor Dev pushed the old man out the back door with all his strength and body weight. In a shadowed dance, they fell together, rolling off the porch onto the ground, while Eli ran toward them.

Lydia was right behind him.

Eli shouted again, reaching them just as Pastor Dev managed to rise into a crouch, his features etched with pain, his hand holding tightly to The Peacemaker's forearm as he tried to wrestle away the gun. Lydia watched in horror as Eli flew into the fray, struggling with the older man. But in the muted moonlight, she couldn't be sure if he was trying to help or hinder Pastor Dev's efforts.

Then The Peacemaker twisted with a grimace, aiming the gun right toward Lydia, with Pastor Dev slapping and hitting at his arm to stop him while Eli stood over him, calling out for him to let go. Dev shouted at Lydia, trying to warn her, then a shot rang out. Seconds passed, then another one followed.

Lydia waited, her eyes squeezed closed, for the pain she was sure would come. The gun had been aimed right at her. But she didn't feel the pain of being shot. Instead, she watched in shock as Eli slumped to the ground.

And then the mountain went still and quiet again.

Dev saw Eli go down, but he also saw The Peacemaker slump over in defeat. Then he heard a soft moan.

"Lydia?" he called out, rushing to her, his hurt leg dragging as he met her beside Eli's still form.

Lydia fell down, her hands touching Eli's face. "He's still breathing," she said, tears streaming down her face. "He's not dead."

Another shot rang out. Dev turned to find The Peacemaker struggling toward him, his gun wobbling in his shaking hand. "I'll kill all of you. I'll kill everyone—"

Then he fell over to the ground, the gun dropping away from his hand. Dev looked down at Eli, then turned to Lydia. "Stay here."

She nodded, her hand rubbing against Eli's arm. "Don't die on me," she said, her tone pleading. "Disciple, don't die on me."

Dev went to The Peacemaker and checked his pulse. He was dead. Then Dev saw the blood streaming from his midsection. In the struggle one of the shots had hit him.

The Peacemaker was dead, and as Dev kneeled over his lifeless body, he prayed that God would grant this bitter old man the peace he had not found on earth.

Then he rushed back to Lydia and Eli. "Eli, can you hear me? Eli?"

Eli moaned, slanted half-shut eyes toward them. "It wasn't me, bro." Then he passed out again.

"We have to do something," Lydia said, her sobs coming hard now. "He saved us, Dev. He saved our lives."

Dev dragged her close, kissing her tears, her hair. "I know, honey, I know. Eli is that kind of man. We'll try, I promise we'll try."

He went about that task, giving Eli first aid, doing what he'd been trained to do when someone went down. He worked on reviving his friend, trying to determine there in the moonlight just how bad the wound was.

"Eli, stay with us," he said over and over, his own tears coming at last. "Eli, you can't die now, do you understand? You can't die." Grasping at how to save his friend, Dev knew there was only one secret left. And he had to tell Eli that secret in order to save him.

He looked over at Lydia, praying that she'd understand why he'd never told her this. Then he grabbed Eli by both arms and held tightly to his friend. "Eli, stay with me. Stay with me, please. Eli, you have to live. You've got a very good reason to live." Then he leaned close. "Eli, you have a son. Do you hear me? You have a son."

Dev heard Lydia's gasp of surprise, saw the glaring brilliance of his secrets and his betrayal there in her confused eyes as she looked up from Eli to him.

And then, he heard the helicopter coming through

the night, its lights shining like a welcome beacon in the moonlight. He heard Kissie's voice calling through the megaphone.

"Hang on down there. Help is on the way."

Reinforcements were here at last.

It wasn't too late for Eli, but Dev wondered if it was way too late for Lydia and him.

She wondered what would happen now.

Three days later, Lydia stood in her bedroom, safe back in Dixon now. Remembering how her parents had met them at the airport in Albany, she dashed at the tears that always seemed nearby these days.

"Lydia, baby," her mother had said, rushing up to touch her, hug her, then touch her again. "I can't believe you're home. We were so worried. No one would tell us—except that you were in some sort of danger and Pastor Dev had you in a safe place while the authorities searched for a killer. Honey, that doesn't make a bit of sense to me."

Her father, ever stoic and stern, had only nodded, hugged her tight, and then backed up, swallowing what surely must have been a big lump in his throat. "Girl, you gave your mama a surefire scare."

She'd tried to explain it all; she'd tried to gloss over everything, sticking to the story that Pastor Dev had suggested way back when this had begun. Yes, they'd been involved in a murder, and yes, they'd been safe. They'd been on a retreat, a quest of sorts, working hard to find the truth while the authorities found the killer. But Lydia knew no one was buying that story.

Yet even when her mother pressed her for the truth, Lydia couldn't put it all into words.

"Just pray for me, Mama," she told her mother last night. "Just pray for Pastor Dev and me."

At her mother's concerned expression, she'd ventured on. "Nothing happened between us. I'm still Lydia, Mama. I'm still your baby girl. And I'm so glad to be home."

Her mother's instincts had hit the nail on the head however. "Something did happen. Something big, I know. You fell in love with each other, didn't you?" Then her mother had opened her arms wide, letting Lydia cry. All of her sorrows, all of her doubts and fears were expunged in that gentle purging.

"He's a good man, Mama. The best. He saved my life. He was always putting me first. I love him."

And that had ended the questions. Even though the whole town was whispering, wondering, comparing notes, Lydia's family had somehow managed to put a shield around her.

Or maybe Pastor Dev had done that.

Right along with avoiding her like the plague.

Now she stood staring up at her poster of Rhett and Scarlett, her heart hurting with such grief that all she wanted to do was curl up with her cat and never leave the safety of this room. But she'd have to get over that notion.

"I had a life," she said as Rhett brushed up against her legs. "I will have a life again."

She'd just have to find another job. Because she couldn't work with him, not now, when her love for him hurt her in every fiber of her being.

He apparently did not love her enough to fight for her, since she hadn't seen him in three days, not since they'd left the airport in separate cars. She with her parents. He with some high-up bishop or elder from the church, and probably from CHAIM.

He had some explaining to do, no doubt.

But all Lydia had were her memories and her nightmares. Memories of his smile and his kisses, nightmares of Eli as he lay near death, and of The Peacemaker, that pitiful old man who apparently had not one ounce of love in his jaded heart, even though he'd masqueraded as a missionary down in South America.

"Forgive him, God," she said now, wishing with all her heart that someone had been able to penetrate that wicked man's soul. "And help Eli, Lord. He's suffered enough. Too much. Help all of us, Lord."

Eli Trudeau had a son. That much she knew. But Pastor Dev hadn't bothered explaining that little tidbit to her. Not on the helicopter ride to a Denver hospital, not in the long hours they'd waited as Eli went through surgery, and not even after Eli had survived and they'd been cleared to come back home.

Now, she had no idea where Pastor Dev was, or Eli, either. CHAIM took care of their own, one way or another.

Lydia grabbed up Rhett, holding him close as she

snuggled her face into his thick fur. "I guess it's just you and me again, Rhett. Another lonely night."

Dropping the purring cat, she decided she'd make some chamomile tea and watch a sappy movie. As if she needed to cry even more. But what else could she do? The man she loved still didn't trust her or love her enough to share everything with her. Maybe he never would.

And even though she knew he loved her back, maybe a man like Pastor Devon Malone just couldn't let go of his warrior's heart long enough to show her that love.

"We'll think about that tomorrow," she said in a long, drawn-out drawl to Rhett. "Won't we, pretty boy?"

And then, the doorbell rang.

Dev stood at the door, his mind reeling with hope and need. He'd tried to stay away, tried to distance himself from Lydia's purity and goodness. He didn't want to taint her anymore. And he couldn't promise her anything else.

He'd been debriefed, analyzed, scrutinized, questioned and reprimanded. He was so tired, so very tired, that he only wanted to curl up on the couch back at his house by the church and sleep for a month. But now that he was standing here, knowing that Lydia was right behind that door, a new energy coursed through him. He had to see her. He had to tell her he loved her.

When she opened the door, her expression full of hope and regret, he took her in like a long drink of pure water. She was wearing a pretty blue floral sleeveless sundress that flared out from her waist in soft, gentle pleats. She was barefoot, her hair caught back in a ponytail, her face devoid of makeup.

She was beautiful.

"Hello," he managed, shifting as he put his hands in his jeans pockets.

"Hello," she whispered, her voice sounding raw and husky.

Her cat made a dangerous meowing sound, the animal's rich green eyes issuing a challenge that clearly spoke of terrible things happening to anyone who dared hurt his owner.

"Hi there, Rhett. Protective as ever, I see." He looked back up at Lydia. "Can I come in?"

"Sure," she said, but her eyes held so much doubt.

Dev wanted to erase that doubt. Once and for all.

"Have a seat," she said, whirling like a ballerina. "I was about to make some hot tea. Want some?"

"No, but I'd take a soda."

She put the teakettle on, then brought him a soft drink. And she sat down in a chair across from him, her body language showing him she wasn't comfortable with him being here.

Hating that, he put the unopened drink down on a rose-patterned coaster and said, "Lydia—"

"How's your wound?"

He wondered to which wound she was referring, his leg or his heart. "Just a little sore and I walk with a limp, but the doctor said I'll be fine in a few weeks." He tried again. "Lydia—"

"Eli has a son," she interrupted, her hands folded in her lap. "I'd really like to hear all about that."

"That's what I came to tell you," he said, dreading this final admission. "It's a long story—"

"But one I need to know," she retorted, her eyes as steely and glistening as copper that had aged to a brilliant green. "It's a blessing for him, at least."

He nodded, opened his drink. Took a long swallow. "First, Eli is doing great. He's going back to Louisiana in a few days. Kissie is going to watch over him. You know, she teamed up with Sally Mae and made the CHAIM team at Eagle Rock track us down."

She nodded. "That's good to hear." Then she held up a hand. "Before you tell me this story, I need to tell you something."

Surprised, Dev said, "Okay."

"Back in Colorado, Eli…he called The Peacemaker grandfather. Do you know anything about that?"

Dev blinked, willed himself to talk. "Eli told me everything. The Peacemaker—his real name was Pierre Savoy—came from a wealthy New Orleans family. His only son, Edward, met and fell in love with Polly Trudeau. Polly got pregnant. Eli." He looked down at his hands. "They never married. Polly was poor and not suitable for Edward in Pierre's eyes, so Pierre enlisted Edward in CHAIM. She never heard from Edward after the baby was born, and Pierre never acknowledged the baby. Then Polly heard that Edward was killed, so she raised her son Eli the best she could and never married again."

He took a long breath, raised his head.

Lydia had tears in her eyes. "That's so sad."

"Yes, it is sad. Eli's mother wanted him to have a better life so she sent him to a community college to get a decent education. That's where Pierre found him and told him about his father and CHAIM. But he sure didn't do it out of love for Eli. More as revenge against his mother and him."

Lydia got up to pace around the room, wiping at her eyes. "So that old man bullied Eli into joining up."

"Yes, and because Eli was starving for any connection to the father he'd never known, he jumped at the chance. And it seems The Peacemaker has had him in his grip off and on through the years since."

"Until South America."

Dev had always admired Lydia's sharp mind. "Yes, until then, when Eli discovered to his dismay that his very own grandfather was behind a huge drug cartel down there. He stumbled right into it—"

"And because The Peacemaker both loved and resented him, the old man decided he had to make Eli suffer."

"Yes, by trying to kill his wife."

Lydia stopped pacing, then looked down at him. "But she didn't die right away. You did tell me that."

"No, she didn't. Eli was AWOL and we had to make a quick decision. She had no other family, because she was an orphan. Eli met her when he was doing some community work at a local children's home. They got married as soon as she turned eighteen. Eli loved her so much, but he thought she was dead and we couldn't find him. So we hid her—without even CHAIM's knowledge—"

"Who is we?"

"Me," he said. "Just me and Kissie and a few other people who were concerned about Eli and about…the baby."

She nodded, held up a hand. "Let me finish this for you. While she lay in a coma, the baby was delivered?"

"Yes. It was the only way. She died shortly after the baby was taken by C-section. It was as if she were waiting for that baby to be born. I wanted to tell Eli, but we couldn't find him. So we decided to hide the baby—to save the child. Eli was so unstable once we did locate him, everyone involved decided the best thing for the child was to keep him hidden. After that, time just passed so quickly, and Scotty was so happy and safe—"

Lydia sank down on her chair, but the teakettle started whistling, causing her to jump up again. Dev got up to follow her across the open room to the kitchen. "Lydia, you have to understand—"

"I do," she said, her attention on making her tea. But Dev could see her hands shaking.

He grabbed her, stopped her with his hands on hers. "I wanted to tell you. Right from the start. But I had to protect Scotty."

She gasped, pulled away, her hands going to her mouth. "Oh, oh, now it all makes perfect sense. Your nephew? Eli's son is your nephew, Scotty?"

"Yes," he said, relief washing over him. "That's it. That's the final truth. My sister has been raising him up North. That's my big secret, the main reason I had to take you on the run with me. I was so afraid someone was trying to get to Scotty—that Eli had found out the truth and was coming after me."

He moved toward her, forcing her hands away from her face, forcing her to look at him. "I was afraid they'd kill you to make me suffer and…that's exactly what Pierre Savoy was trying to do. That's what he did to Eli. I couldn't let that happen to Scotty. That little boy means the world to me. And he's innocent. He's innocent, Lydia."

He hadn't realized he was crying until she reached up to touch her fingers to his tears. Dev grabbed her hand, kissing her fingers, hoping against hope that she would forgive him. "I'm so sorry. For everything. Please, Lydia, I need you to understand and to forgive me. Please?"

Lydia felt the warmth of his hands on hers, felt the love shining in his eyes. "This is…incredible," she said, her heart hurting for Eli and for his child.

And for this man who'd taken on the burden of protecting both of them, and her, too. "Does Eli know now?"

Dev looked down at their joined hands. "Yes, he does. He knows everything. He's bitter and hurting, but he did thank me for saving his child." He shook his head. "He kept quoting one of the Beatitudes— 'Blessed are the merciful, for they shall obtain mercy.' He said to tell you thanks for that one."

Lydia's heart opened wide in a prayer for Eli

Trudeau. He had been listening to her prayers that night up on the ridge after all. "What's he going to do now?"

Dev backed away, then rolled a hand down his face. "First, he has to get better. He's still recuperating, and it'll be a while before he can travel again."

"And when he's well?"

He turned to face her, his expression full of hope. "He'll go and find his son, I'm sure."

"Then it will truly be over?"

"I hope so. I'm done for now. I'm out of CHAIM for good."

She moved toward him, wanting to make sure he was real, needing to see his honesty. "And...no one else will come to kill us?"

"No. That's all been taken care of. The authorities in both the United States and Rio Branco are on the case now. It's truly over." He gave her a wry smile. "Things might actually get back to normal."

"Normal?" She shook her head. "Not really. I have to find another job."

"Why?"

She couldn't help but savor the solid fear in his eyes while she asked God to put forgiveness in her heart. And because she was a different person now, she decided to be a bit more assertive and bold in telling him the truth.

"Because it's not proper—what with me being in love with my boss. Rumors are already flying left and right around here."

He lowered his head as he came toward her. Then

he tugged her into his arms. "I can fix the rumors, I promise."

"I've heard your promises before, remember?"

She saw the hurt passing through his eyes, but she had to know she could count on him.

He leaned his forehead against hers, then backed up to stare at her. "I know you have, and after that night in New Orleans, I decided I wouldn't make any more promises to you unless I knew I could deliver on those promises."

Lydia gazed up at him, her breath in her throat. "And can you? Deliver now, I mean?"

"I plan on it," he said as he leaned down to kiss her. "You know, I always have a plan."

Breathless and suddenly giddy with hope, she smiled. "What is your plan?"

"I plan to marry the woman I love," he said, fresh tears forming in his blue eyes. "I plan to make you my wife, and I plan to preach the word of God right here in our church, and I plan to have children with you, and grow old with you and—"

He let out a yelp of pain. "Your cat just bit my leg."

She slapped at his shirt, grinning through her own tears. "Rhett, oh, he's just making sure you can live up to all those promises and plans."

"I can," he said. "I will." Then he gave her a serious look. "Lydia, will you forgive me for all that I've done to you? For all the things I've withheld from you, including my heart?"

"I will."

"And, will you marry me?"

"I will."

His expression changed from fatigued and unsure to content and relaxed. "Thank you, God," he said, lifting his words to the heavens in a prayer. "Thank you, Father."

Then he looked back down at her. "You are so amazing, and I love you so much."

Lydia silently thanked God, too, for the words she'd always longed to hear. Then she fell into his arms, all of her doubts melting in a pool of sweet warmth. "I love you, too, Pastor Dev."

"You can call me Dev now for sure," he said into her ear.

"You'll always be Pastor Dev to me," she replied. "Always. Even when I'm Mrs. Devon Malone and life is perfectly normal again." Then she touched a hand to his face. "Even if life is never normal again."

"I can live with that," he said. "I'm so glad God put you in my life. And…I like normal. A lot."

Then he whirled her around in his arms, and they both laughed and cried together.

While Rhett the cat watched, purring away in delight.

* * * * *

*Don't miss Lenora Worth's next
Inspirational Romance,
DEADLY TEXAS ROSE,
available January 2008
from Love Inspired Suspense.*

Dear Reader,

This story was a departure for me. I have this secret love of action-adventure movies and stories, so it was a thrill to write one of my own. When I was about seven, I told my mother I wanted to be a secret agent. She told me that was fine, but I might get shot. That didn't sound very good, so I just pretended to be a spy in my yard and the surrounding country. Thankfully, I changed my mind about being a secret agent when I realized I was born to write books.

Maybe you have a secret dream you've never pursued. I hope you follow your heart and work toward that dream. Lydia's only dream was to marry Pastor Devon Malone. But when she discovered that the man she loved had a secret, she was both devastated and intrigued. Devon wanted the same thing as Lydia—a simple, faith-filled life away from all the pain and suffering he'd seen. But before either of them could find their dream, they had to work together to stop the bad guys.

With God's grace and guidance, we can survive and become stronger and better. I hope that you will find it in your heart to let God be your guide, no matter your dreams.

Until next time, may the angels watch over you. Always.

Lenora Worth

QUESTIONS FOR DISCUSSION

1. How did Lydia react when she realized Pastor Dev wasn't the man she believed him to be? Have you ever thought you knew someone, only to find out you really didn't?

2. What was the one thing that remained the same for Lydia throughout this story? Why was her faith so important to her?

3. Why did Devon feel it necessary to keep his past life a secret? Do you think he truly wanted to become a better man?

4. Why was Devon so torn between the past and the present? How did Lydia help him to overcome his torment?

5. Do you believe Devon was an honorable man? Do you think a person can be honorable even when that person isn't completely honest?

6. How did Devon's feelings for Lydia change? Do you believe he loved her all the time, but had to see her in a different light before he could acknowledge that love?

7. How did Lydia's idea of a proper Christian change through this story? Have you ever been surprised by other Christians?

8. Why did Devon keep the final truth from Lydia? Do you believe he was protecting his friend Eli, or himself?

9. Do you believe some Christians use their faith as an excuse for being dishonest or criminal? Have you ever known someone like The Peace-maker?

10. Do you believe Eli is redeemable? Have you ever known someone who was tormented by the past, but found solace in Christ?

REQUEST YOUR FREE BOOKS!

2 FREE RIVETING INSPIRATIONAL NOVELS PLUS 2 FREE MYSTERY GIFTS

Love Inspired®
SUSPENSE

YES! Please send me 2 FREE Love Inspired® Suspense novels and my 2 FREE mystery gifts. After receiving them, if I don't wish to receive any more books, I can return the shipping statement marked "cancel." If I don't cancel, I will receive 4 brand-new novels every month and be billed just $3.99 per book in the U.S. or $4.74 per book in Canada, plus 25¢ shipping and handling per book and applicable taxes, if any*. That's a savings of 20% off the cover price! I understand that accepting the 2 free books and gifts places me under no obligation to buy anything. I can always return a shipment and cancel at any time. Even if I never buy another book from Steeple Hill, the two free books and gifts are mine to keep forever.

123 IDN EL5H   323 IDN ELQH

Name	(PLEASE PRINT)	
Address		Apt. #
City	State/Prov.	Zip/Postal Code

Signature (if under 18, a parent or guardian must sign)

Order online at www.LoveInspiredSuspense.com

Or mail to Steeple Hill Reader Service™:

IN U.S.A.: P.O. Box 1867, Buffalo, NY 14240-1867
IN CANADA: P.O. Box 609, Fort Erie, Ontario L2A 5X3

Not valid to current Love Inspired Suspense subscribers.

Want to try two free books from another series?
Call 1-800-873-8635 or visit www.morefreebooks.com

* Terms and prices subject to change without notice. NY residents add applicable sales tax. Canadian residents will be charged applicable provincial taxes and GST. This offer is limited to one order per household. All orders subject to approval. Credit or debit balances in a customer's account(s) may be offset by any other outstanding balance owed by or to the customer. Please allow 4 to 6 weeks for delivery.

Your Privacy: Steeple Hill is committed to protecting your privacy. Our Privacy Policy is available online at www.eHarlequin.com or upon request from the Reader Service. From time to time we make our lists of customers available to reputable firms who may have a product or service of interest to you. If you would prefer we not share your name and address, please check here. ☐

LISUS07

Love Inspired® SUSPENSE

TITLES AVAILABLE NEXT MONTH

Don't miss these four stories in October

SHADOWS IN THE MIRROR by Linda Hall
Her aunt warned her against returning to Burlington, but Marylee Simson had to know why her parents' very existence seemed shrouded in mystery...and whether handsome Evan Baxter could be linked to the tragic accident that had claimed them.

BURIED SECRETS by Margaret Daley
Fresh from her grandfather's funeral, Maggie Somers was stunned to find his home ransacked and her family's nemesis, Zach Collier, amid the wreckage. Could she believe his warning that the thieves would certainly target her next?

FROM THE ASHES by Sharon Mignerey
Angela London was haunted by her dark past. Now a guide-dog trainer working with former football star Brian Ramsey, she needed to thwart a vengeful enemy to protect her newfound happiness.

BAYOU JUSTICE by Robin Caroll
With an angry past dividing their families, CoCo LeBlanc's discovery of her former fiancé's father's body in the bayou put her name at the top of the suspect list. Working with her ex to clear both their names, could she survive the Cajun killer's next attack?

LISCNM0907